Puff of Time

Puff of Time

SMALL FABLES
&
TALL TALES

THOMAS TIMMINS

ZOËTOWN MEDIA
HAYDENVILLE, MA

ISBN 978-0-9970287-3-7
Printed in the United States of America

Published by Zoëtown® Media
Zoëtown is a registered trademark of Zoëtown Media.
Haydenville, MA
www.thomastimmins.com

Book and cover design by Maureen Moore, Booksmyth Press
www.thebooksmythpress.com

BOOKS BY THOMAS TIMMINS

Novels

Blood Medicine

The Special Fruit Company

Down at the River

The Hour Between One and Two (Trilogy)

Aphrodisiac for an Angel

Short Fiction

Puff of Time

Visions of My Other Self

Desert Dusk Music

Graphic Verse Novel

Zom

Poetry

I Was Just Laughing

Likings for Shadows

Buddhist Breathing in America

For Andrea, Peter, John

Contents

Mother O'Day and Natalie O'Night

When the late afternoon wind flung itself up the canyon chasing the clouds, the mariachi band folded up its chairs and stretched a royal blue velvet drape across the seats of the wagon.

Old Mother O'Day climbed aboard carrying on her wrist her canary named "Olalalu." At eighty-five, with the benefit of only her alchemical creams and herbs, the old woman remained as beautiful as any former movie star,

Settled on her pillow on the buckboard seat, she clucked to the ponies. As they clip-clopped into the desert behind town, her guitarist lover sitting beside her sang the Sonoran fantasy, "Amor del Muerte."

The old lady waved a scarlet silk scarf and the sun dropped below the horizon, splashing bloody and yolky streaks into the cornflower sky. Sliding under the guitarist's fingers and across the well of the guitar, a canyon breeze strummed long bass notes, announcing old Mother O'Day's seductive daughter, Natalie O'Night. An uninhibited silver moon slid through silky pale cirrus clouds slowly as a held breath, little by little revealing O'Night's opulent curves, finally baring all in the cabernet sky, unveiled to lovers and the loveless alike.

My mother darned socks

In charge not only of our souls, but our soles, she darned thousands of socks for her gaggle of children. Her perfect hand-stitch outdid any machine because, once darned, no sock allowed itself a rip, a tear, a rent, not out of fear, but from pride. Sometimes that made me sad. I'd look at my socks and think if only unmendable holes would sprout somewhere, I'd get a new pair. But my darned socks lived forever, giving my soles a taste of immortality every morning when I'd slip the crooked but vigilant tubes onto my little feet.

When I grew, I got my new socks–good school socks, better church stockings, calf-high baseball socks, thick football socks. For years, the basket beside my mother's sewing chair overflowed with socks but she didn't darn these new ones. And I left my immortal darned socks behind in childhood.

Somewhere, right now, dozens of the socks my mother darned are lolling around, footless, amusing themselves with memories of the joyous afternoons we spent racing shoeless, skidding across the polished splinter-free floors of my grade school gym. I can see them smiling their saggy smiles when they recall us squishing, stocking-footed, in the garden, leaving sock marks, my mother's darning a singular stamp on heel prints in the black muds of the Plains.

Deep in the holds

Deep in the holds of a container ship passing through the Panama Canal locks, mice and bananas whisper clues to each other.

"If you stop smiling," a gray mouse tells a green-as-a-seasick-novice banana, "they'll love you as much as those bulby papayas and leave off with the spray."

Without really listening to the mouse—mice natter on constantly there in the dark—the mellow banana rhymes. "Smooth seas, no cheese; deep swells, rotten smells; high waves, cat behaves."

Before long, the ripening preservative haze settles over the racks and rows of banana bunches, dampening all conversation.

Should we worry about the mouse?

No. He buries himself in the corner while bananas in bunches, each one smiling wide as the whole canal, take the fog on their bellies, dauntless prows conquering any weather.

Later, when the mist clears, the mouse says, "Thanks, pal. Didn't feel a thing. I love ya, even if they don't." The blissful banana, model patience, nods and mumbles, "No problem," and proceeds to yellow with age.

Gone Missing

Ninety-four, she went missing from ordinary life on the fourteenth floor, down the elevator, out the door, without shoes, cane, hearing aids, or even the pearls Danny gave her what, seventy years before?

When she didn't return, nobody knew where she'd gone, or if she intended to stay away for long. Her cell phone buzzed on the bedside table where she left it , vibrating the TV remote every time it rang.

Lulu Sweet, the missing woman's neighbor, rang up the daughter the next morning and sounded the alarm. "Did you know your mother stayed out all night last night–it was cold here–at her age?"

The girl dropped the phone and sped as fast as a car could drive through LA at midday, and when she arrived, another day had passed, but she was just in time to greet her mother who rolled in the apartment door on fat white wheels, sitting in a glistening pink enamel and chrome wheelchair.

She snapped at the daughter, who worried too much, "Did you think I lost all my good sense?" By Elder-Bus, she'd gone wheelchair shopping the next town over and she liked the Indy 500 Turbo model so much, she'd bought the franchise for her building.

"Five hundred old ladies and a dozen geezers? All living too long, like me? I'll make a killing," she said. She invited everyone to a show in the courtyard where she had Henrietta, the desk clerk, demonstrate wheelies, spin sharp turns around blind corners without the slightest tilt to the seat, and, best of all, activate the sensor bars that enveloped the carts automatically if the driver forgot where she was and rolled too close to something.

The old woman made her first cash sale and took orders for fifteen of the hot machines. "C'mon," she said, "whoever can make it. Let's celebrate. When we go out, we're going like nobody ever did."

The daughter called the doctor, wondering if her mother needed a sedative or twenty-four hour care to keep her out of trouble. "Look. What can she do, worst case," the doctor said, "kill herself?" "Yes," the girl groaned. "Who's life is it?" the doctor said. "Hers to make me miserable," she said. "OK, I'll call in a prescription for you, a nice new drug that will make you happy as a jaybird." "You want me singing at my mother's funeral?" She slammed the phone down and turned to retrieve her mom.

In the distance, a fleet of wheelchairs approached the barrier at the entry by the guardhouse. "Either let us out, Jimmy," the old gal shouted, "or we're gonna blast on through. We don't watch CNN for nothing."

The gate rose and the old ladies paraded toward the mall, white hair and shawls flying behind them, enameled hot pink wheel chairs glistening in the late afternoon sun. As they rolled down the street, they resembled a flock of low-flying flamingos cruising the shore with nothing better to do until sunset.

The old-time gangster rap

He's a good kid. He does a good job, too.

Yeah, he does a good job. Too bad he fucked up, Ronnie.

He's a good kid.

He fucked up, Ronnie.

C'mon, give him a chance. Can't you see he's young. He's trying.

Ronnie, what the fuck did you say? Anybody who fucks up, anybody who hurts me or mine, that's it. Besides, I can't set no presidents.

But ....

Ronnie, do I hear you right? Do you wanna go with him? Don't fuck up, Ronnie.

Fuck you, fuckhead! He's my kid!

Blam! Blam!

Two men fall dead.

The kid picks up the guns.

Record-breaking flight of one Vergillus Magnimus

In Fargo, North Dakota, March 26, 2003

For thirty-six years Dr. Anderson studied bugs, in Fargo, North Dakota, in Jakarta, Indonesia, in Christchurch, New Zealand. This morning, his career's crowning, a single vergillus magnimus, your common barn fly, flew six kilometers around and around and around the Flight Mill at the USDA headquarters in Fargo.

The little buzzer winged onward in silence, seeking the imaginary gray light far down the infinite tunnel. Though bred to be the Über-fly among minions of flies that pester the world for putrefaction to crop their larvae in, it couldn't cling for long to the steel sides of its night. A ordinary insect, perhaps female, the fly persevered the full four hours it took to traverse nearly four miles.

Could it have flown further? Dr. Anderson doesn't know. We non-scientists don't know. We may never know, but what must horrify us to our very withers is that, if a one hundred fifty pound human were to run for four hours with that fly's speed and endurance, that human would circumscribe the globe ten times.

No wonder bugs scare us. We should fear them. Jeff Goldblum, rethink your character in the movie The Fly—one human fly clone would rule the world by pure libido.

Dr. Anderson admits the awful catch in his

fly-species cloning plans: If you invite one fly to a party, it
shows up in hordes—all looking alike, all super-extroverts
wanting to dance, their buzz so gossipy they hurl themselves
unasked into everybody's secret shit.

The alien

Unlike those with the slanted skim-green eyes, the zipper lips, and the smudge of a nose, my friend, the alien, has a warm human face—clear brown eyes, a nose that says "It's me," and plump maroon lips. She's not married and lives in a hut in the woods, but otherwise, you wouldn't suspect she's the kind who would steal our women and children for transport to LG-631 for their hideous experiments.

No, the real danger she presents is that she's a teacher, seducing the minds of youth. She advocates preposterous "truths," such as laughing is humanity's true purpose in the universe, far beyond loving and thinking; the U.N. should establish the Galactic University of Body Language to stimulate communication among all sentient species; and, when all people can read and write, human evolution will resume. Clever as a racoon, she's the biggest joker on the faculty, not someone the authorities worry about.

I told her the only thing that bothered me about her origin in the Sirius system is that she can't really understand us or empathize with our miseries and dreams the way even my dog can.

She giggled and pinched my ear, saying, "Hey, did you ever notice those wrinkles back here?"

I felt behind my ear and said, "No."

Her eyes sparkling, she said, "Interstellar telepathy

vanes, for sure. We don't grow them in our quadrant, but they're common in the Betelgeuse group. Did you ever ask yourself where you came from?"

When she said that, I wanted to kiss her.

Night music

Outside the movie theater, a thin black man wearing a slouch-brimmed hat leans against the building, trumpet to his lips, ploughing through the foggy night with blasts and runs that fade at the corner of the building.

A woman with long brown hair and a stocky man, both dressed in black shirts, white pants—off-duty waiters, bartenders, line cooks—smoke cigarillos and talk on a bench under a Granada streetlight.

His phone to one ear, a lit flashlight his other hand, a fast-striding young man slashes across the night's gloom.

On the next street over, in her tiny flat, a tromp d'loeil painter, fled from her fat, bearded piano player husband, sits on the edge of her tub admiring her new sapphire toe-ring.

A church bell in the valley of my memory rings twice, then the chime slides down the curtain of fog and thuds into silence in the grass.

Fukushima Floozy

They arrived just before the searing afternoon winds blew out of the dry alley beside the café, with it endless, coughing of dust.

America's favorite kind of tea, Iced Tea, was the house specialty that afternoon. At 2:17, Akiko had arrived on the Greyhound. That called for a stiff double espresso.

Akiko opened her purse and pulled out a brown medicine bottle with a rubber squeeze bulb tip.

He said "What's that?"

"It's not your Mormon Tea," she said. Tilting her head back and opening her mouth, she squeezed three drops between her lips. "Echinacea tincture," she said. "I brought it from the Ukraine. We call it Fukushima Floozy." She glanced at him and shrugged. "Want some?"

He nodded and held out his coffee cup, sure he couldn't handle it straight. She dripped a little in and he sipped. Not bad. Wouldn't make the Starbucks top ten, but it had a nice alcohol bite.

Akiko interrupted. "Don't joke about it," she snapped. "If you Americans took life more seriously, you'd forget about your money for nothing and have fun without killing yourselves and everybody else."

He finished his coffee and set the espresso cup on the gray marbled counter. "Can I carry your bags? We have a fifteen minute walk to the cemetery."

He lifted her suitcase. It must have weighed eighty

pounds. "Jesus," he said. "Haven't they invented wheels over there yet?"

Akiko everted her fleshy lower lip then grinned. "That's better. You're almost funny. Like my uncle. The one who still lives not far away. He raises chickens and feeds them the Floozy. You should taste those chicken eggs. They're so tiny and delicious we call them Fukushima Caviar."

A career change

William returned from California after seventeen years of clipping hedges and planting succulents. If he hadn't lost his shears over the side of the Bay hydrofoil, he might have stayed for another seventeen.

Back East, he bought a camera to start a new career.

"It's all about phases," Clarita, his prospective teacher, told him during the interview. They sat on a gray dock downcoast from Bar Harbor watching seagulls bicker over spilled lobster bait. "You shoot a hundred shots, then another, maybe improving your technique, maybe trying something new every hundred or so."

"I used to be into flowers," William said. "Trees, bushes, all green growing. Right now, I'm thinking about a radical change. I've got this idea about the Civil War's effect on the Maine fishing industry."

Clarita pitched a stone at the gulls. They spread their wings and skittered and hopped across the splintered planks but didn't rise.

"Watch this," William said and ran down the dock. The gulls scattered to the masts and bowsprits of the sailboats tied close by, peering at him from the corners of glassy eyes. "Did you get that?" Bob asked her.

She let the camera hang against her chest from a braided leather lanyard. "You running? The birds flying? Chum dropping from the hooked beaks? I shot a shadow on

the dock of the gull floating overhead with its wings spread,
waiting for you to stop fooling around."

"Digital?"

"35 mill. Digital's for tourists. I thought you were
serious."

"Color?"

"Black and white. I mean, shades of gray and blue."

"You're hired," William said. "Let's get to work."

Debate about trees

This morning I saw the first hummingbird dart into the treetops next door where the trees look more like thirty-foot tall bushes that manage to stay vertical by hanging on an invisible tether to the sky. These trees grow boughs just thick enough to support flat needles of leaves pointed up, tugged by transparent fibers. In their reedy flow, the trees might be cousins of eastern weeping willows, only this branch of the family has no sorrowful limbs sagging, no drooping tendency at all, only their joyful arising toward the sky.

Rebecca, my graduate student friend tells me, "'Weeping' and 'arising' and 'joyful' are human behaviors—trees don't do those things."

She's right. Perhaps it's more accurate, more scientifically correct to say these willow trees have 'adapted.'

She laughed while she picked her teeth with a weed stalk, "No, Paolo, that's another crazy human idea."

"OK. You have to admit something's happening. How about "The trees are sunning themselves?'"

"Now you're getting somewhere." She sniffed a peach-colored rose. and offered me a whiff.

"This is the life," I said, stretching in the sun and looking for a nice shady spot to lie down in. Intellectual confrontations exhaust me.

Cookies

He saw her coming up the sidewalk and he ran to the door wearing his last year's Halloween vampire mask.

His mother opened the door and came home from work. Her mouth opened wide and, tilting her head, she leaned against the door jamb.

"Who are you?" she said "Have you seen my little boy?"

The boy turned around and ran to the kitchen where he sat at the table, tapping his glass with a spoon.

"Oh," his mother said, standing wide-eyed beside the refrigerator. "If I had a kiss from some sweet stranger, I know just where to find the oatmeal cookies."

"Do they have raisins?" the vampire asked. "You know we like raisins better than blood."

"Pecans, too," she said, picking him up, and puckering her lips. "Toasted pecans."

"Chocolate chips?" he asked.

"Chocolate chips," she said as she raised the mask and tasted the buttery batter of his little mouth.

Her bestiary

She rolled up her window shade and when he tapped on the glass, she glared at him with empty eyes he'd never seen before. Streetlights sifted through the tinted glass painting her face with shadows of bars. Behind her, large lithe bodies shifted in the dark, oily fur glistening in the downtown night glow. The window glass muffled throaty animal moans and he backed away from the car, unnerved by icy gleams in the shapes of teeth.

He heard the doors click as she locked herself in with animals in her personal cage on wheels, and her car chugged out of the parking spot, hauling off a whole train of creatures growling and hooting in fear, or anger, or joy, he couldn't tell.

She's afraid, he thought, on the run, escaping with her bestiary, concealing them inside the night before the men with nets and chains show up from the animal farm.

He shouted after the speeding car, "I admit it – I have some nets but I've never owned a whip." He yelled as loud as he could, "I'll throw the nets away!" Three blocks away her tail-lights blinked out around the corner.

"Too late," he muttered, hopping on his Vespa and buzzing the opposite way toward home where his lizards, three cats, a ferret, and his angelfish aquarium waited for him in the whispering dark.

Watching the movie about Pollack
with a prosperous painter

"Where shall we sit?"

"I have a bum leg," she said.

"Okay, you can sit on the aisle."

After they settled in, he asked, "How did you cut your fingers?"

"You notice everything," she replied, sliding her band-aided fingers under her sleeve, out of sight.

"You probably don't want any popcorn, do you?"

"You're right. They always put too much butter on it here."

"How was your day?"

"I got a lot of work done."

"What are you working on?"

"Oh, I'm just starting. I was making progress till this guy came over. He's always coming over when I'm trying to work."

"Your neighbor?"

"No. He's a sculptur. Says he needs a break and likes to look at my work in progress. He doesn't know anything about painting."

He dug deep into his conversational atlas to come up with some comment to warm her up. "This is supposed to be a good movie," he said.

"That's what they say. I don't really like Pollack, but I thought I should see it anyway."

She was a famous painter but he'd never heard of

her. Mostly corporate investors buy my work, she'd said.

Changing the subject, he said, "Some people say I look like Matt Damon," he said, feeling the first-date dance spun out of control.

"Maybe," she said. "I can see it a little bit. A fatter one."

He frowned and sighed.

"I don't mean you're fat," she said, then looked at the maroon drapes above the proscenium in the classic opera house now non-profit movie theater.

The curtains drew back and the music began dripping the painter's compulsions across the screen.

They watched, neither moving until, when the movie ended, they shifted in their seats and stayed for the credits. She hated the movie, she said. She already knew the ending.

He loved it, he said. But then, he admitted he loved every movie he sees, if it didn't bore him.

Outside, she climbed into her pickup, the one she'd bought to haul her wall-sized paintings, and said, "See you."

"Maybe we'll bump into each other sometime," he said. He banged on the side rail of her truck bed with his palm as she pulled away. She slammed on the brake and rolled down her window.

"What was that?"

"You didn't hit me," he said.

"I know," she said, and shot away.

I would have liked to look at her paintings, he thought. To see what people pay big money for these days.

Saved by TV futbol

I met Lori in Guatamala, her last stop on a year-long around the world tour. As we walked down a dusty street at sunset, a group of men gathered around us. With their greased-back hair and tight clothes, the men could have been Villaistas, Zapatistas, or the boys from the back lot finally getting a call. They gripped our shoulders and shoved us toward a door in an adobe storefront.

Inside the store, a half a dozen barber chairs lined up in front of a wall-length mirror. The men, all moustachioed and gruff, muttered as they pushed us into chairs at opposite ends of the room.

I struggled, but two or three held my arms and legs while another one strapped a band around my forehead and clipped an electrode to my right earlobe. I noticed they gave Lori the same kind of attention. She whimpered, but they ignored her.

A shock tore through my earlobe and raked across my skull, under my skin. My head nearly broke open with pain. Just as suddenly, it subsided. The men let me go and wandered outside. I heard one say "TV" and another say "futbol."

I sat, my ear attached to the electric wires, wondering why they'd tortured me, braced for more shocks. None came. I looked through the yellow shadows toward Lori. She slept with her head tilted to one side. Her electrode dangled like an earring.

Turning around, I saw my red sweating face in the mirror. As I stared into my eyes, I realized it wasn't only torture. Someone was watching us. I picked up a wooden brush from the counter and threw it against the mirror. It cracked. I threw the jar of green disinfectant and the mirror shivered, then the whole wall buckled and crashed to the floor.

Lori woke up and said, Stop it. They'll come back.

Let's go, I said. There's nobody here but us.

We ran to the front door and stopped in the archway. The men knelt in a circle rolling dice, silently focused on the center of their circle. We slid around the edge of the building and spotted our car, a new blue Mazda blanketed with yellow dust. We climbed in and I found the key in its hiding place in a secret slit along the window molding.

I looked at Lori. Her filthy face was smeared with blood and streaks of sweat. She sobbed and jerked her chin at me, her green eyes fiery. She grabbed my hand and forced me to insert the ignition key. I turned it and we drove off, slowly at first, so we wouldn't raise a dust cloud. By the time we crossed the hill to San Cristobal, we'd turned ourselves into shadows and disappeared.

Wrong number

"Hello and a fine morning to you," Josh chirped.

Someone–it had to be a friend–called at five a.m. on this of all mornings. Today, he and Elliot, his drummer, would tell Maxine Garvity "No. No more. That's all she wrote."

They'd vanish forever from the dismal set on left rear stage of the Cash Flow Lounge where he twanged his Martin B-75, an original and the only asset he owned, and Elliot percussed and cymballed the air behind magicians popping cards, hypnotists embarrassing the audience, and women teasing tired German Shepherds or a couple of matted Angora rabbits animals into strangely human cries that everyone howled at and Josh tried to harmonize with.

And today he and Elliot would fly–

So when the caller asked in a muffled voice "Is Franklin there?" Josh startled.

"Who? Who?"

"Franklin."

Smiling broadly at the caller's innocent mistake, Josh sighed. "No. No, I'm sorry. Wrong number, buddy."

The voice insisted, "You don't know that and my name ain't Buddy."

Josh cringed. His mood puckered slightly at the rim of what had been a fully-inflated hugely optimistic wide open blue sky kind of appreciation of all and everything. No way would he let that happen on this of all days.

Josh hung up gently, bent over the bedside table and yanked the jack out of the dismal hotel's phone, severing any possible random or intentional connection while, wide awake now, he planned his entrance into the club: Would she beg him and Elliot to stay? How much was it worth to her if they did?

Ah, who cares? Money can't keep me down he muttered and pulled the pillow over his head. The club didn't open till four.

In the steamy woods

Emily had never felt more alone. Cicadas buzzed and crackled from the trees. All around the two of them, the leaves dripped with afternoon rain.

They breathed hot fog.

No human sounds penetrated the forest. South Carolina in July–the sky hung like moss.

His hand closed on her wrist.

She twitched at the touch of his icy fingers sizzling on her sticky skin. She moaned silently.

Why did I get myself into this?

His fingers dug into her wrist bones until they ached.

She wanted to pull away, but she was afraid to. If she did, Mikey might panic and fall into a puddle of tears, slowing them to a stop. She'd have to coax him and coddle him through the shadowy woods home to the video game their mother'd promised them for going to the store to bring her a pack of those stinking Virginia Slims.

Richard Brautigan, western writer

Richard Brautigan had to talk, needed listeners to feel his thoughts. So, when he was alone, he saddled up and rode his typewriter, stopping to pick up apostles, penguins and sexy girls, spouting tall tales through his handlebar moustache all the way to his hometown, iDeath, where he never once said "I wish I had a glass of watermelon juice."

Facebook

Semi-sad news arrived by email tonight.

Jolene had fallen ill with an old-fashioned ague nobody remembers the antidote for and Bill couldn't find his car keys.

Jim Simpson, their e-neighbor and only remaining Pole in our community– not that it matters except he knows how to raise the juiciest cucumbers–Jim sent me the sad tag, tho he calls his Facebook communiques 'emissives,' because the word 'email' tastes like a cigarette stubbed out on a sidewalk and, he claims, only the hopelessly addicted would pick up and put such a word in his mouth.

I wrote back saying Tell Bill I'll drive to the store. What does he need?

Later that evening, Jim replied: A nice bouquet will do.

I searched until I found gladiolas at MarketDay.com and shipped off an e-bouquet to Jim's.

A little while later–time means nothing when you live from emissive to emissive–Jim wrote I forwarded your flowers. Jo and Bill say thanks and how long will they last?

I hit reply immediately. Don't worry, I wrote, my fingers thinking for me. My wife says don't worry how long. Enjoy them now.

Then Jim wrote back almost before my finger lifted off the Send command, snooping with his e-telepathic mind. I didn't know you had a wife.

Uh oh, I said to myself. It's starting again. Until I wrote that emissive, I didn't have a wife. Very happily married, I wrote Jim. She travels a lot. How about you? Hoping I'd bored him.

I did. No, Jim wrote sometime later that week. I stay home a lot. By the way, your wife is right. Those glads last forever. Smart gal you got there.

Oh no, I said aloud as I clicked Reply, surrendering my fingers to avoiding the truth which is I'll never get married. Unless it's an online thing. That one would always last somewhere in the cloud, like the gladiolas, even when we forgot about each other. Like we would. Who remembers anything anyway these days?

Brewmeister's video

My best friend and freelance partner, Ishmael Al Ra-Badeen, and I were talking about his plan to change his name to Izzy Shapiro when we pulled up outside the big old house.

We'd driven across the new SkyLiner tracks to meet with Carl Stockenhausenfreihandundlandsfrau, the famous Braumeister of East Bavaria, retired. I got dizzy for a moment from trying to pronounce their names. They're on to something out in California where middle and last names have dropped off into that five-mile deep Pacific canyon.

allboozeallthetime.com—abatt—had hired us to get a video interview of the old brewmaster regaling us about his artistic heritage. They planned to broadcast our work on their *Toast of the Day* feature.

We got out of the car and took the three deep breaths we always take before an interview. The earth under my feet was right where it belonged. We walked up to the sagging front porch, its paint chipped off, exposed black siding.

"If this house were a dog, it would be a Dalmation," I told Ishmael.

"Call me Izzy," he said. "I want to get a feel for it before I file the papers."

"Okay, Izzy," I said as we climbed the rickety steps.

Carl was ready for us. Sitting at a scarred wooden trestle table that looked like he'd brought it from a medieval castle in Bavaria, Carl nodded to three mugs of beer.

"Greetings," he said, raising his mug to the camera in Izzy's hand.

"Guten tag," we said in harmony, sitting down to wet our whistles. The beer was pretty good, but I'd expected something a little less hoppy.

Before I could ask my first question, Carl leaned forward and almost shouted. "Number one, he said, don't count on anything or anybody. Number two, just because you do a good job, don't think your problems are solved."

We nodded, both of us grinning. The interview was off to a good start. If he kept spouting old world wisdom, and toasting us, we might even have an archive piece. We'd get paid a royalty every time somebody dragged it up.

Carl raised his mug again, tipped it toward us, then drained it. He slammed it down and stood up. "Finish up, boys. That's it." He turned toward the door.

I knew I had to rescue the interview somehow. I said, "Wait, Carl. This is your shot. Think of all the women who won't be able to resist that drippy mustache of yours."

I was already tipsy so maybe my judgment failed me, or maybe my intuition took over. Walt, the producer, was probably right when he reviewed the piece later. "You dissed the old boy. Nice job."

On the porch and in the video, Carl glowered at me. He picked up his empty mug, swinging it toward me like a mace. I stumbled back down the stairs, catching myself before I landed on my duff in Carl's weedy yard. Izzy, ever the imperturbable Bedouin, captured every red blotch and fierce gleam on Carl's face. We had a hit on our hands. We knew it the minute Carl growled.

"Hunde. Ich schlagen Sie!"

His berserker growl would instill fear and laughs in the minds of abatt members for years to come.

Calm, all of a sudden, Carl said, "Drink with me, boys," pacified by our offer of the imported bottle of Austrian schnaps we gave him. "Any time. But leave that verdammte camera in das Auto."

It wasn't long before abatt developed and ran an animated series starring a character named Der Brewmeister. Izzy negotiated a nice commission for us, cutting Carl into the deal. But Carl never gave us another interview.

Mrs. Peroni's hummingbird recipe

As usual, Mrs. Peroni sang to her hummingbirds at noon, announcing their floral treat of the day. Yesterday was lemon blossom, today rockrose. Tomorrow and every Tuesday, the ruby-throats feasted on morning glory dew.

"How did you ever tame them?" I asked as we watched about fifty birds darting and scissoring in and out of her feeder. We stood beside the little stream we shared as a border between our acreages. Half-acreages, really. But with maples and a brook. Darn fine living back in those days. Genteel.

Mrs. Peroni glared at me. "For one thing," she said, throwing her arms up in disgust, "they're not tame. How many times do I have to tell you?"

I smiled and stammered, "I'm sorry." I felt certain she'd never told me that. But why would I contradict her now? She was about to say more, perhaps to reveal a secret of our suburban universe. And I should start an argument?

With a warning note in her voice, she said, "Those little critters are wild as ky-oats. Fierce as teeny tigers. Don't get too close." She leaned across the rippling water, as if now she'd whisper the end of the neighborhood enigma in my ear. "I use my grandma's maple syrup and blackstrap molasses recipe. Blend them 50-50, stir a teaspoon into a cup of water, add the dab of flower essence, and voila!"

I nodded, waiting for more. Then it came.

"Every hummingbird falls for something sweet. Just like every man."

I pursed my lips, annoyed at her using hummingbirds to pronounce another cliché about men. Other than that, I admit, I had a crush on Mrs. Peroni. It was her oyster-grey hair and dense black eyebrows and something about those wrinkles beside her sparkling eyes. I like a woman who speaks her mind, too.

We listened to the brook's fidgeting and tinkling. It splashed tiny drops on our toes. Time passed agreeably, as it usually did in those days.

Then I said, "Is that it?"

Leaning further toward me, staring me in the eye, she said, "That's it. Remember it."

"I will," I said, and I did. How could I forget? I remember it still, one hundred twenty nine years later when hummingbirds the size of chipmunks rule my yard. Good thing I have Mrs. Peroni's grandma's recipe. I carry a bucketful on a stick and when the hummingbirds flutter around my head, I swing the bucket back and forth like a sugar lantern.

The hummingbirds can't resist. They swill the sweet juice and with their bellies full, they leave me alone. I think I have a good chance of taming them. When I do, I'll invite Mrs. Peroni over to thank her for her recipe and surprise her with my tame hummingbirds. I heard she's living up Mysterioso canyon growing peaches and plums and making jam.

I can't make it down the the Farmer's Market any more but if I could, I'd buy a case.

Dream shifting

In a loud whisper, the aged hypnotist commanded "Go back into your dream state." Immediately, all three clients, but not the dog, recalled their latest dream.

Dory felt in her stomach the queasiness as she watched her old boyfriend chainsaw through her refrigerator door seeking barbecue-flavored yogurt. Mrs. Antrim forgot her upcoming surgery and let herself sail off in the exhilaration of a moonlit flight over a twinkling prairie, and shameless old Noble Harris squirmed in his chair, a steely erection vaulting forth just like earlier that morning.

Satisfied he'd entranced them all, the weathered hypnotist lowered his voice, pitching it even softer. "Be brave now," he said, and paused, expecting the dreamers to drift deeper into the synthetic silence. "Be brave... strong...go for what...you want."

Obedient as always, Dory imagined a new gas grill, pork chops, and John and Susan over for dinner. The old boyfriend became a mere outline of an arm clutching a yogurt cup. Mrs. Antrim flew on, riding gravity's wake like an angel, and arced south, toward the Caribbean, while poor, brazen Mr. Harris groaned in his sleep: That green-eyed anchor woman from Channel Six wouldn't unbutton her blouse. Mr. Harris nearly burst a vein in his temple, imagining her reaching toward him, trembling, but her fingers barely rippled the surface of the glass, his dream director never able to convince her to wiggle them through the screen of his new fifty-six inch Sony TV.

The elderly hypnotist forgot where he was and when he woke up, he knocked over the cup of yogurt on his TV table while he switched from Discovery Virgin Islands to the local six o'clock news. His own trousers bulged, for which he was always grateful.

Encounter on the Robert Frost Trail

Hiking up Mt. Toby on Sunday to view the Valley from the 70 foot fire tower on a glorious December day, I said "Global warming global shmorming," quoting the presidential candidate, pleased with the heat, pleased with the amber and emerald woods, pleased with my companion.

Slipping down the steep, shaded, north side of the mountain on a spur off the Robert Frost trail, we met a poet climbing up. Unlike us and any other hiker we'd seen, he wore his work clothes, a blue oxford button-down shirt, gray v-necked sweater, chinos, vibram-soled brown leather shoes.

We hiked with sticks to brace ourselves when we crossed greasy patches of wet leaves, but the poet stepped firmly and slowly, oblivious to the slick trail, secured by gravity in his determined uphill stride.

He told us he gave up his practice of the genre of haiku in 1997. In 1998, he moved to Hartford to be with a woman and to manage a bookstore. He helped her sell her house and her son called him father. After breaking up with him four times in one year, she succeeded in granting him his full bad luck.

I was carrying a tiny nest I'd found on the other side of the mountain. A band of white birch bark stripes wound around its base like a scarf. I pointed out the skill in the bird's beak that peeled the bark into narrow strips the precise width and length for weaving into the nest. The former haiku poet stared at the nest as if wishing he could crawl in and let me carry him home with us.

He'd suffered Hartford for too long since the breakup, now he had to move someplace green. Another poet friend of his, a man who turned all of his Vietnam into poetry and had done very well for himself, had longed to move back to green New England from plastic southern California. It took him three years but he made it. This gave hope to our poet.

We said good-bye to the poet after discussing these hard times and learning that he'd begun to see twisted auras around a lot of people's heads. When he gave us his business card with the address of his bookstore on Gallows Hill he said, See that address? I should have known. He trudged on up and we sauntered down with our sticks and empty nest while composing melancholy haiku in his honor.

> chicks long fledged,
> empty bird's nest
> pilfered by human hands

and

> climbing down the mountain trail
> holding an empty nest
> we met a sad poet

Laughing at our dreary little poems, we gave up, deciding to leave the haiku to our former haiku poet friend, while

> strolling around the iced-in pond
> at the foot of the mountain
> holding hands

Eighty-eight

He rolled over in bed looking for a cool spot to lay his sunburned face on. The sound of the late night TV annoyed him even more than the sense of stuffiness in the room.

"Eighty-eight more nights – I'm outta here," he groaned.

"Shut the fuck up, Rafe," barked Tiny Tracy, his six foot six cellmate. "Some of us need our beauty sleep."

"Tiny. I'll miss you, too. Don't worry. When you get out, I'll give you a job."

"I hate donuts!"

"It ain't donuts! It's a bagel shop! You'll love 'em."

"Shut up and go to sleep, Rafe. Don't make me think about holes."

Dream come true

Sarah couldn't believe it.

She held her breath.

She couldn't stop shaking.

He was so strong and beautiful.

She'd never smelled anybody so intoxicating.

Sam was finally climbing into her bed.

She'd dreamed of this for a month, ever since her birthday when she met him at Dr. Devore's puppy nursery and she'd spotted him in the litter of precious newborn cocker spaniels.

The mother of the lie

Do you ever feel your throat close around your words just when you were about to make the point that the main reason they should hire you is that you know how to make money and you're happy to make it for them?

When of course you're happy to make it for them if they give you plenty of room to do it however you want and don't bother you with their petty ego needs to tell you what to do.

When you're about to lie to save yourself from homelessness and they can't know that or out you go.

Surfing

My son insisted he'd rather surf the Rock in the north Atlantic in November without a wet suit than go to work at a job hated.

"What about hyperthermia?" I asked.

"What about asphyxiation?" he replied. "What about claustrophobia? Schizophrenia?"

He had a ready wit. I took out my handkerchief and, always modeling good behavior for my children, I sneezed into it.

"Salud." He smiled while I blew. "Gesundheit."

"What about ...?" Thinking for a moment, as my son continued his litany of diseases, I fell into a shallow trance like the one you feel when listening to Gregorian monks chant. "What about carpal tunnel syndrome of the mind? What about following orders to the grave? What about getting fitted for the torturers' mask?"

"Son," I said, "Those are damn serious charges."

He sipped his Pacifico beer and leaned close. "What about dying at your desk and nobody finds you until they smell your corpse stinking?"

I stood up and dug into my pocket. "Here," I said, handing over my credit card, "buy yourself a wet suit. Remember to get a cap and booties, too."

A wide grin slid across his face, exposing his teeth. Speaking as gracefully as a surfboard skimming the lip of a six-foot wave, he said, "Pops, when the water warms up, you come on out with me and give it a try. I'll show you how. It's all about the water."

The president's soul

The president sold his soul to a fisherman named Pete from Fall River who had only the small price of his drowned father's leaky cod-fishing boat to offer.

The president said, "Don't worry, Pete, I'll give you the senior discount. Just happens three carriers dry-docked in my home port and my dad's cat ranch has gone bonkers with sales to the rat-soaked home owners of Bath. I'll cut you in on the deal. Call it the Peace Reprieve, the Cod Man's Bounty, anything you want," he said as he pocketed the grizzled seaman's cash.

"By the way," he added, "what plans do you have for that paltry scrap of imagination you just bought with your life savings?"

Alert as a gull at dawn, Pete considered. "Well, sir," he said, his gimlet eyes on the cavity in the president's forehead where his third eye never grew in, "first thing, I throw it into the hospital's laundry."

The president wrinkled his brow.

"Only way in this town to clean out the bloodstains and the shadows soaked down into the weave," Pete explained. "Then, I guess, I'll sell it on ebay. Some collector out there's gotta need another president's soul. What with how famous you are and all, I'm hoping for a record bid. Bigger than the last president's, that's for sure."

The president smiled, glad to hear he'd hold another world record, for a while. "Good luck, Pete," he said and as the valet fetched the vaunted Hummer. "Where I live, stupid beats smart but clever beats stupid. How about one more game of rock scissors paper?"

Pete whipped his hand behind his back.

In a split second, the president faced an unexpected battle.

"Hold the car, Masters," the president said to his chauffeur, his legs spread and bent. "I got a war to win."

Get it done by Elvis's birthday

Two days after New Year's, the choice assignment arrived on my desk. They'd supply me with my own truck and trailer, the choice of colors was mine – and they expected me to finish by Elvis's birthday next week.

I called up Jim at the station and asked "Why Elvis's?" He thought it over for a few minutes as I waited, drinking some of that new tea named Thunderbolt that had a picture of Zeus slamming lightning bolt after lightning bolt toward the earth aimed at what looked like New York City. I was surprised that the store even carried such a blasphemous package in these days of terrorist retributions. I drank the tea feeling a bit conspiritorial, sneaking glances over my shoulder to see if anyone was spying on me.

"It's OK, Buddy." Jim said. My name is Luis but Jim calls everybody Buddy. It must be easier than remembering names like Tso-chin, Sendze, Wilfredo, Halimanaranand, Pedreszhnov, and the other people on the crew. Jim calls the women Buddy, too.

"You can have till Martin Luther King's Birthday. It's not as big as Elvis's, but hell, as long as they're cleaned up by the next holiday, the people won't care." That gave me another good week.

I told him thanks and went out to get my gear. I'm felt sure I had plenty of time to pick up all the trees. The town only has about 500 blocks to it, if you lay them side to side. Say, 4 trees a block or even 5. That's only a couple of thousand trees to toss into my trailer and cart them off to the Mulcher.

I love the smell of pine and balsam. When those Norwegian firs leak that sweet sap onto my coveralls, I can count on having a special night with Teresa. With the fir smell on me, she thinks I'm a woodsman come to save her from the trolls she has to work with all day.

When I unloaded the first couple of dozen trees at the Mulcher, Mulbroskiwicz ran out of his shack screaming at me.

"Get dat fuckin shit off Big M! She's shut down for da day. What're ya tryin t'do? Jesus Christ." He had nicknames for everybody, too, only his were some variation of a last name that only he could make sense of. My last name is Juarecito. The Spanish J must have inspired him.

Now, I hate to see a trashy yard or disorganized work area. I don't mind a little dust, but disorder pisses me off. If I see my Christmas trees piled up like garbage when they should be chopped and diced into little chips for the garden, I'm likely to lose my good attitude. "Mully, what shall I do with them? I'll have two, three hundred trees before day's over. You gotta start her up."

"Yeah, yeah. What th' fuck d'you care? It's my fuckin machine!" Mully crossed his arms and jutted his jaw. I couldn't speak. I fumed. I was tempted to pick up one of the driest trees and lash him with it. I could see his face bleeding while he dug needles out of his skin and eyes. My face felt hot. When I didn't say anything, a big grin tore across his face.

"Tell ya what. I don't wantcha ta bust a pipe in yer head. Leave the trees. Them damn pines gum up the blades. Jus fer you, I'm gonna sharpen her teeth and give her a good reamin with oil. I got a barrel a used engine oil from the dump trucks – she slurps it like it was cum!" He laughed as if his joke was funny.

"I leave the trees," I said, "you chip em today?"

"Yeah, don worry, Bosco. We take care of it. Just leave em there." Mully turned away.

"Mully," I called, "we both got jobs to do. If we both do our jobs, we're both happy. The boss is happy. The town is happy."

Mully looked back. "Jesus Christ. D'ya think I give a shit who's happy?" He slammed the door to his shack. The door muffled his next curse. "Hehu Hi!"

Mully's mood was so foul he was likely to chip his own hand off if I made him run the trees through the Mulcher now. I decided to call the boss and leave a progress report after work, but not to get Mully in trouble. If I didn't have any place to stash my trees, how could I finish the job even by Martin Luther King's birthday?

That's a paid holiday. Our next day off is not till Good Friday. The union got us the afternoon off, sharp at twelve so we can go to church and pray we don't go to hell, or if we do, Jesus will come and get us.

I've screwed up enough in my life to qualify for hell, I guess, but I ain't bad. Mully, he ain't bad either but he seems like he's in hell today. Way he talks to me makes me want to get the pitchfork outta my truck and slam it into his gut a few times. He'd be calling for Jesus then all right.

In Maggie's mind's eye

Across the canyon, houses jut off the ridge, threatening to lift up in a flock and soar downward over the horse barn where the Rodriguez family keeps their 23-year-old stallion, Amigo Rojo, and raises golden pheasants and Vietnamese pigs.

But who in her right mind, even noticing the delicacy of coastal hills, would ever imagine the shimmering stucco houses planted on their red perches as serious threats of flight?

Maggie would not only imagine it, she'd feel it and see it. Eminently sane since she stopped fearing her father around the time her mother stopped drinking again, she climbed the 14 steps to the gallery set like a widow's walk a top the family's ranch house roof and looked upward, into the valley and the houses propped along its walls.

As she watched, in broad daylight, stones popped out of the side hills, dripping like fat globules, sparse rain spit on the tile roofs of barn and house. She heard the message of movement from above.

In an instant, she saw in her mind's eye and heard in her mind's ear and smelled in her mind's nose, and felt in her fleshly stomach, the pale blocky suburban houses gathering themselves, grinding free of crumbling foundations, and rising straight up a few inches over pungent sage smoldering.

Tilting, the houses leaned forward, tensing for somersaults across the chaparral, tipping into graceless dives down gravity's chute, when Maggie saw in her mind's eye a wrinkle in the air. A fast, hot zephyr howled up the canyon, bearing up the houses all together on open palms of wind. In her mind's nose she sniffed the metallic bank of fresh kelp washed ashore. She heard in her mind's ear timbers dressed in stone groaning as the houses lifted and blew off toward the ocean. She felt in her true heart the lightening of the burden on the hills as it all disappeared from over Maggie's head before she could blink.

Maggie climbed back down the 14 steps from the roof into the yard calling her favorite pig. "Let's go, Winnie. We'll find some high mesa to explore."

In her mind's eye, she saw a broad meadow spreading far off toward snow-capped mountains and in her mind's ear she heard her pony Winnie's contented snorting as he followed her through a fragrant field bursting with chicory, clover, and yellow asters and little red flowers glowing everywhere underfoot.

Puff of time

A sixty-year puff of time, a glowing cloud of time floated alone in a pale turquoise sky.

Watching sunset from the lakeshore, he thought, "Sixty years sure makes a small cloud."

The cloud hung low in the west, purpling with the oncoming night, until an enormous gray cumulus poured out of the north and scooped up the shimmery little cloud into its misty belly.

Leonard Cohen and the birthday rake

"Really, Mr. Jacobs. Do you need another rake?"

I had to ask the tall jowly fellow. It's not usually our customer service policy to resist our customers' purchases, even the looniest ones. Folly is always at the heart of most buying in our little store here in the backcountry of southern British Columbia.

But his wife had called a few minutes earlier and said, "Humor him. It's his birthday."

I said "Fine," and I meant it.

At **68**, he could afford to buy himself anything for sale in the whole town, including the most expensive house, for example. That was the old Feingold estate with its orchards and stables and three guesthouses each with its own pool and streams everywhere you looked. The estate sat on the edge of Balders Woods which backed up on the national park and on clear night the aurora borealis looked like a reflection of the Milky Way in a speckled black mirror.

"How about one of our new French coffee presses?" I said in a spirit of reconciliation, sensing that I'd offended him.

"No way, Jimmy. I need this rake. Keeps me in shape raking leaves off my clay court before I have a game. Besides, I like to make patterns in the clay."

I knew where he was headed with this. I settled back against the gun case and waited for the latest rendition of his years in the zendo with Leonard Cohen.

"You know," he said, "Leonard wrote his most beautiful songs in the dust. Then he'd laugh, if you could call that cackle a laugh, and he rake out the words."

"How about that?" I said.

"Leonard told me his favorite writing instrument bar none was a ten-tine oak-handled garden rake.

"Five solid couplets in one flat head – a whole song Leonard used to say. I never forget that. I buy one every year. Jimmy, you're the only shop around that carries these oak-handles. Forget those molded plastic mutants. They couldn't scratch a flat fart of a half-note on a sidewalk."

Mr. Jacobs hoisted his rake onto his shoulder and turned to leave.

I lifted my hand a said, with some urgency, "Mr. Jacobs ..." but I stopped myself.

He waited. "Yes?"

I recovered and smiled. "Happy birthday. And happy raking."

He whirled and pushed the door handle, the head of the rake barely missing the new solar photovoltaic elkhorn chandalier we had on special that week. The door slammed on the way out, shaking the Timex watches we displayed on the shelf, just like every other satisfied customer did when they left.

I gotta fix that, I thought. I was glad I kept my mouth shut about the rake Mr. Jacobs bought. I was going to tell him he'd miscounted the tines. It had only nine. But who was I to tell him, Leonard Cohen's scratching-in-the-dust pal like an old rooster. Besides, isn't there some famous poem out there with nine lines?

I seemed to remember Ms. Jazorski in high school standing in her tight white cashmere sweater reading one to us. Nine lines, I'm sure she said that. Rhyming.
Hey, lines rhymes with tines.

I'll have to tell that one to Mr. Jacobs when he comes in next fall for his birthday rake.

Headfall

Twenty-two years old.

He's changing his first son's diaper, one year after the war ended. If he'd served in that war and lost fate's flip of the death coin, this baby would never have been squalling and squirming on the bassinet.

His boy padded his tiny wrinkled feet up and down against the rubber pad and punched his fat arms into the air. The father marveled at the activity of his son, more vigorous than his friend's one year old. The baby gurgles. To the man, his son looks like he's swimming in the yellow afternoon sunlight that's alive in the room.

The father bent down to look for a cloth to wipe the yellow creamy odorless poop from his boy's bottom and tight little balls, forgetting to put his hand on the silky soft belly.

Just as he stood up, he saw the boy's heels disappear over the end of the bassinet.

Instantaneously, he heard the wooden clunk and a howl of pain and helplessness and rage.

O my God.

He dashed around the bassinet, catching his toe on the leg and pitching it over toward the baby. He slapped at it, snagging it and flipping it away. It lands behind him, collapsing far away from the crying infant.

He picks up his son, cradling his head in his hand.

Please please please.

The baby's tears wet his father's cheeks. He screamed

again, then turned his head toward his father's chest.

Sobbing, the father held the boy up to look at him. The baby's lips drooling lips trembled, his wet glazed brown eyes stared at his father.

Would he forgive him? He was okay, nothing broken. He must have hit his forehead, but it's still round. A little whiter there in the middle?

No damage done. But could he forgive him? He'd probably never remember falling, unless something happened to his neck. He seemed fine.

Should they take him to the doctor? No, I'll just watch him. If he eats all right when she comes home, then I won't worry. I won't even have to tell her. She'll know.

All I can do is wait and see.

A crimson welt formed on the baby's forehead. A vertical ridge rose just above his dark eyes where he'd slammed his face into the gap between the floorboards. The ridge darkened as his father watched. He kissed all around it and rocked the boy back and forth, back and forth, soothing both of them.

Don't let there be a scar. Let him be okay. Please.

A cloud came over and dimmed the room. The dad started walking in a circle, then he found the bottle and brought the cold, sticky nipple to the boys lips.

The boy ignored it as his father slid the soft rubber back and forth. A few drops of milk leaked onto his mouth. He licked them with his bird's tongue, then nibbled at the nipple, then swallowed the tip and began to suck. He sucked until the bottle went dry. He cried a few times, glancing up at his father out of half-closed eyes, then let them fall, and he slept.

The father sighed.

Poinsettia Planting

Overnight, the snow disappeared from Paula's yard, as if she and Manuel had planned it. There he was, already outside, poking around in the garden with a stick. How long had they been together? And he was still the handsomest man she knew, and so good to her.

He'd done the breakfast dishes for years–ever since she started school again–those wonderful years–but this morning he left them stacked in the sink. She leaned against the counter, burying her arms in the hot, soapy water, sighing.

Ah, mother, here is where you soaked. Your cure for your arthritis, the same place you got it, like daddy's hair of the dog.

Paula quickly pulled her slender fingers and hands out of the water and dried them off. She remoted the CD player on to 'Five Centuries of Classical Flute,' and opened the back door so Manuel could listen to the flutes singing like robins. She missed them so much. Thank God spring was back.

Manuel turned and smiled, waving his stick. "Mrs. Ortiz, good morning. I have found the perfect spot for your poinsettia bush. Right here, between the jade and the agave. Plenty of light."

She waved back and said, "Fine, dear, if you think so. But aren't you worried about another snowstorm?"

He scratched temple and shrugged. "I never saw snow over here by the coast."

He was joking, of course. This year they'd had more snow than the winter of '87 when they could ski right off the back porch. "Whatever you say, honey. It will look nice there, all red and green. I can think about Christmas every time I look at it."

Seal

"Did you notice that rock sticking up out of the water?"

Mike and his friend watched the seashore pass through the bus window.

"Did you see the seal laying on it?"

"Nah. I didn't look very close."

His friend leaned over to Mike and reached out his hand.

"Let me have the remote, will ya? Or else you switch it. It's time for the NBA Today on ESPN."

"No problem. I'm tired of this Discovery Channel anyway. I wish I'd seen the seal. I'd like to see a one in person someday. At the real ocean."

The Osprey
in Five Chinese elements

For Debbie Gunther

In the backcountry, on the edge of a remote glacier lake, I kicked the ball as hard and high as I could. Down the yellow dirt road, my friend waited near the trees to catch it. Round as a soccer ball, heavy as a rugby ball, the color of a basketball, the ball rose in a steep arch, slicing west under the wind toward a marsh dense with reeds and cattails. The ball dropped into the pocket he'd made of his hands held at his belly. He gently tucked it to his chest and the breeze died down.

Three short, stocky men dashed up the road to meet him as if they'd been waiting in the oaks for the action to begin. The three fen men formed a wedge, the ancient Spartan strike position, and plunged off the road with serious business on their faces, disappearing into the silence of the slough.

Within minutes, an osprey rose above the water beyond the reeds, winging out over luminous blue. As if frightened by something it had discovered on the shore – perhaps the fen men had surprised it at a feed – the osprey flew so high I nearly lost sight of it's white belly, a pale smudge on the clear afternoon sky.

Two other ospreys, sleek as cloud shadows, closed in, joining the first. The three ospreys stalled in the air, raptors conferring like coincidental scouts or old monks. Then, the first osprey turned around and dove back toward the shore.

Once before, while I rode my bicycle through the Lakes country, an osprey and its companion flew over me. Then from hundreds of yards away, one touched wingtips with its mate and wheeled back over the fields to fly with me. It floated nearby, hanging in the Prairie wind watching me, until a mile later, satisfied, it swung away toward its vanished companion.

When the osprey reached the shore and disappeared behind the bog, the breeze rose again, scraping across bent reeds and carrying scents of algae and mud to the little rise I stood on. At the crest of the hill, not far from me, a majestic woman appeared. I knew I'd entered a dream and my shadow lengthened on the road behind me.

Dressed in a long scarlet silk robe bordered with the golden brocade a Shakespearean queen would wear, jangling gold hoop bracelets, and a gold chain lying heavy around her neck, she walked directly toward me. The sun behind her head obscured her face. The breeze lifted her hair off her shoulders, playing with it. Had I stumbled on some medieval reenactment?

When she reached me, I saw that she was only twenty-five or so. She asked me if I'd seen her servants. They'd been fishing in a skiff, she said, and she fell asleep on the shore. She needed to get home, but her horse had wandered off, too. I told her I'd give her a lift in my Durango but we had to wait until my friend came back. Had she noticed him by the lake? She heard something, she said. It woke her up. But she thought it was only the osprey crying.

Forgiveness

For Wendy Foxmyn

The celebrants, or maybe penitents, though I for one wasn't up for doing penance, gathered on the beach on a cool late morning. I could definitely get into the forgiveness, but paying in the flesh wasn't part of the deal. It never has been, though to tell the truth, sometimes I think I deserve it. I know I do.

I'm lucky I had the upbringing I had. My old man never hit me once. My mother? Well, dear thing. She always gave me the second chance. The third. Fourth. She still hasn't given up, even if she has no idea what my life is all about.

I'm not the nicest guy, even when I try. Like some people constantly get sick, or have bad luck, or good luck, I'm always hurting somebody, not that I want to. I'm good at it, and cold, but I never go out looking for someone to trash. Because of that – hey, I'm a realist – I could get slammed even if I can't help myself. Revenge is human. Rosh Hashana is the highlight of my year. My armor. My invisible shield for the next 365 days.

"This is the highlight of my year," I muttered to the woman next to me, Gloria Spelman... or Solberg... Simpson... Gloria, anyway. I felt proud to know I'd be forgiven that day for some pretty major sins, just by writing them down and sailing them off into the dissolving sea.

How powerful words are, especially when you treat them like magic trash and they clean the mess inside your head.

"Me, too," Gloria said. "It's right up there with my birthday, Christmas, the 4th of July, my wedding anniversary, my second wedding, that is." She scrabbled around in her black purse hanging like a flight bag off her shoulder.

Overhead the sun wanted to shove the clouds aside. You could see them drop lower to avoid its reach. We stood on the hard-packed sand a few dozen yards under a misty fog. A few feet from our toes the water foamed up then slid back, teasing, or timid. Either way, it left a dull oily spoor on the beach.

Gloria took out a legal pad and began scrawling furiously. While she wrote she said, "Yeah, another great day is the anniversary of my divorce, my first divorce. And the only one so far. Groundhog's day because spring is around the corner, and Halloween." She stopped writing and looked at me.

"I love to dress up," I said. "Last year I went as a parrot. At first people thought I was funny, but they got annoyed pretty fast. Everywhere I went in the room, like a wing of silence flapped in my face. So I took off my nose and mimicked their masks. When they laughed, I laughed, and pretty soon, everybody was roaring. Until I put my nose back on. Then it went silent again. Then I took it off. All night I was like conductor of voices and laughter with my beak the baton."

As she rambled on, I turned my back to concentrate on my sins. Well, one big one is what I really needed forgiveness for. I drove Wilson into bankruptcy, he had a heart attack, his wife left him for a judge, and now he's shackled to the IRS for the rest of his life. I had to do it. It was him or me and I had a lot of people to look after.

The real sin was when he called me and asked by for a holdover loan. $25,000. Nothing. But I laughed and hung up on him. I couldn't help myself. That's why I think I'll be forgiven. I can't say I won't do something stupid or cruel again, but I won't mean it. It's too late now to do anything for Wilson anyway. I'd try but it wouldn't help. I heard he's in a wheelchair. Pity. He's only 55 or so.

I'd nearly finished writing my sins in calligraphic script on special vellum I bought just for today. I'd planned to lay the paper face-up on the wave so the Lord could be sure to read it before the water washed it away. You don't have to put your signature or anything. Every sin is personal and this is the one time you can trust that the right guy will get your message without you having to shout. Of course, Gloria interrupted.

"Now you brought it up," Gloria said, her nasally voice pricking my hopeful thoughts, "the highlight thing? My Aunt Edna's vision day – that's the highlight of a lifetime. If there's any magic in this world, Edna proved it. She saw the exact numbers sequence on the parking ticket she got when she doubled-parked in front of Bigby's. She won $50,000 and saved all of it to have a party every year on that very day."

I was in no mood to reminisce with Gloria. Compared to her shimmering highlight days, mine were dry stones in the shade. But they were mine. I watched my sin slip down the beach and turn gray, soaked in the steely water. I watched it until it sank, then I raised my eyes.

Dozens of people were up to their waists in the water, ripping page after page out of fat notebooks. Some made paper airplanes out of them, some crumpled them into raggedy balls, some ripped the papers into tiny shreds and sprinkled them like confetti around their bodies. Everybody looked pretty happy.

Gloria slipped out of her shoes off and rolled down her stockings when I turned away and hiked back to the pier. Back to another year of not being able to help myself. I smiled. Couldn't help myself being happy, either.

The sesame seed army

After taking an extra walk today, the dog sleeps on the sunroom floor an hour before he usually drops off. He ignores or doesn't hear the tiny crackling of sesame seeds roasting in a pan.

White seeds pop, fly up and fall on the stove top like shells shot wildly in combat between the Confederate wooden spoon and the Yankee cast iron skillet.

The conscripts in the sesame infantry, drafted out of cool lives settled in remote valleys of the refrigerator, have lost all respect for military protocol. Using common sense, the only weapon they can trust, they break ranks and sweep across the searing plains of the skillet, their blue and gray caps popping off their heads as they dance on fiery metal, fleeing the circling spoon.

The heat of the retreat scorches their bare foreheads. Soon, the erratic armies brown and glisten with effort and lie down in exhaustion. An invisible cloud of scorched oil perfumes the kitchen sky over the battle.

The war ends in stalemate. The pan cools off, the spoon lies down. As usual, the foot soldiers on both sides suffer and lose the only things they had that mattered.

The seeds disappear into the unmarked graves of mouths, remembered for a few minutes for the smoky savor of their going and the crisp sesame skins wasted in the corners of the skillet, useless as tiny crumpled caps.

The play

Too tired to join in, the old lady who used to work at the bookstore watched me with soft eyes while I packed and wrapped and stacked carton after carton of old books.

The buxom young assistant behind her, short auburn hair shining under the library fluorescents, ordered, "Take them to the other side of the stage. Then see the chief. He'll tell you what to do next."

I approached the chief in his office, surprised that such a young man with green and purple spiked hair led the conservative librarians. He told me to wait. He'd be with me soon. He had to finish with somebody else.

Across the street, at the YMCA, my sons dived into green water. The older boy swam across the pool underwater, holding his breath. The younger sat in the hot tub, smiling, relaxing for once. I'd asked the older boy to come with me to the library after swimming–I had a role for him to a play.

A long open wooden box lined with a black velvet cloth that flowed over the sides lay on the floor in front of the check-out desk. My son, a contented smile on his face, climbed in, lay face down and with his eyes closed, pretended to sleep, waiting, trusting.

From then on the play deteriorated. A rough, stocky man carrying a thick staff, burst through the door from the children's room shouting, "Let's get real!" He raised his staff and turned his shoulders like a home run hitter and swung it, smashing it against box.

A wave of silence broke over the room.

Breathless, I knelt by my son, lifting and hugging his body to my chest. "You all right?" I whispered.

"Yeah. No problem," he said.

I screamed "Arrest him! Call the cops! Stop him!" The man stood quietly, his part done, watching the crowd of readers approach, circling him.

My son breathed easily. I almost laid him down so I could grab the staff and pound the silent man's head. The chief came out of his office. All the patrons looked up from their books. Everybody was watching. They're still watching.

Bad news

On a sparkling October afternoon, two boys sit on the grass beside the garden.

The pudgy red-haired boy was not yet five years old. He smiled and rolled a soccer ball back and forth between his ankles. His brother was eight, thin, holding himself straight up and still. His eyes darted from his father to his mother and back.

Their mother crouched next to them, the knees of her jeans muddied from her harvesting tomatoes and spreading compost.

Their father paced, a lump in his throat.

He said, "I have some bad news." He barely got the words out.

Tears began to roll down the cheeks of his older son.

"I guess you know your mom and I haven't been getting along lately."

The father sat down between the boys and reached his arm around their shoulders, hugging them to his sides.

The younger boy looked at his mother, signaling her with his hand to join the family hug. The older boy buried his face in his dad's chest.

"I'm moving to a new house, boys. By myself. I won't be living here anymore."

The man felt his son's warm tears soaking into his t-shirt, wetting his skin.

The boys' mother knelt down next to them on the grass.

The younger boy slid out from under his dad's arm and leaned toward his mother. She pulled him onto her lap.

By now, the man was crying openly while a silent flood of tears spilled out of the mother's blue eyes. The older son sobbed and heaved against his father.

The red-haired boy scanned his family, his face pale. His eyes narrowed, an uncomfortable smile tugging at his mouth, he said to his mother, "Can we go play ball now?"

Gefilte fish

A whole school of gefilte fish arrived at the seder table, on separate plates. Each finless, scaleless parcel the size of a small child's hand came veiled under a leaf of romaine, hidden as naturally as in a pond, or bay, or the whatever deeps the gefiltes long for at times like these when they find themselves under drying lights, starring in the minor scene between the triumphant final cry of the Haggadah, "Let's eat!" and the entree of the braised lamb.

If the little gefiltes could rewrite their parts in the ancient drama, they'd return the Passover feast to the dreamy dark and icy waters where they could slip away through kingdoms of salt and crushed apples, nose chopped walnuts while acting like forensic specialists of the exposed floor of the Red Sea, looking for Moses' Stolen Tablets of the Ten Commandments. In their living Seder dream, the gefilte have no deadline and no one waiting for their reports, because, really, the only evidence of crime they would find would be the faint moos of the satisfied diners and the spoony rustling of horseradish, and besides, nobody would care.

The crickets' dire message

Germaine claimed he could never get lonesome enough to stop worrying about how much is enough, or the conditions and quantities, worldwide, of potable water in 2027. Especially in early fall, when the streams dry up and all night every cricket in the moist temperate part of the Northern Hemisphere practices its commencement speech from Cricket Toastmasters. Crickets love water and depend on it so it's no surprise that they repeat one message: "Open the taps, water your yard."

Here in the desert, I don't hear any crickets, but when Germaine imitated them, I told him I couldn't agree more with their insight about water. I'll never water my gravel yard, no matter how long I live in Phoenix.

Germaine stretched out on his bed and chirped and sawed away, pretending his noises were crickets. "They soothe me, Joel. They're my babbling brook, my green noise machine."

I said good night and closed my eyes, drifting off to the alpha beat of my battery-run travel clock. My off-grid travel clock always beeps me awake just at the instant I set it for, so I never worry now about missing anything I'm supposed to do, long before I'm used to rising, like when I have to pick up somebody from the airport.

As usual, I expect another deep, long night's sleep because I never worry about brown and blackouts though they stun my electric clock into the electronic infancy. When it waves its ruddy digital arms flashing silent cranky cries "12:00 12:00 12:00 12:00" until I pick it up and change it with tenderness in my fingertips and the patience of a childless heart to "12:01."

Brunch music

Wearing a sleeveless gown the color of champagne, the beautiful harpist with the long wavy chestnut hair stroked her medieval harp. Her fingers were long, of course, and her small biceps were round but firm. The uplifting music came from her elbows, the fulcrum of precise caresses.

Without warning, the beautiful harpist with the long wavy hair stopped playing and abandoned her instrument to the empty stage. My friend, Jules, who obviously had fallen in love with more than the music, looked at the forlorn harp and said, "I'm hungry. It's time for brunch." She left the theater in search of the ideal bagel and freshest lox.

"Go to Braunstein's," I called, "if you want the best sesame in town." I noticed five or six people get up from the back rows and leave the theater, following Jules.

I waited five minutes, expecting to hear backstage supplications, ignoring my own hunger pains. The audience murmured, then one irate woman stood up in front of me, and waved her sharp elbows like snapped harp strings. That was it.

If I hurried, I could beat the crowd to Braunsteins. Bev, the owner and my friend, might be there. If she was I could cadge a Gaulois and commiserate about the spoiled prima donnas we knew. She has had a lot of turnover lately. I told her she should at least give the ladies free bagels to take home. After all, she can't sell them as seconds and maintain her reputation for the freshest in town.

Ambush

She propped the 30.30 on a rock, then lay down to sight the rifle.

Her daddy hadn't taught her to hunt for nothing. All those squirrels and pheasants. She knew what she was doing.

Her target would emerge from the barn in a few minutes. He was more dedicated to the goats than he'd ever been to her. Never something this big. Yet.

She rested in the sun, her eyes focused on the barn door, her gun stretched deadly in front of her face. Harmless birds twittered from the scraggly trees around her. Cicadas chirped away like rusty razor blades scraping paint off the storm windows.

She'd spent many a sweltering summer afternoon chipping and brushing paint peels the year her daddy paid her $5.00 an hour helping him fix up the place. Her main friends then had been the birds and the bugs. She loved the ladybugs and the dragon flies most of all.

Where was he? He was supposed to leave the barn every afternoon by three. She looked at her watch. 2:59.

Almost time. Her worries would soon be over. She relaxed a little in the heat, remembering how she was supposed to breathe-slow and calm-before she squeezed the trigger. A fine sweat spread across her neck and dripped down between her breasts.

She looked at her watch. 3:01.

Where was he? Goddam it. I have to get back in 14

minutes or they start looking for me. He better hurry up. I'm tempted to get up and go find him. Show it to him right in his face and let him have it.

She took a few deep breaths.

Okay. Five more minutes. Then I'll rush the barn.

She noticed that the birds had stopped singing. The cicadas sawed and slashed away at the afternoon, but without the comforting bird trills she began to lose her patience. She got up on her knees and pulled the gun into the crook of her arm.

Bonnie, I've been looking everywhere for you. We missed you at lunch. You must be really hungry and thirsty. Come on, let's get us a lemonade.

She stared at him.

How did he get behind me? Shit. I'll just take him out now.

She raised gun, aiming at his scrawny belly hiding behind the pukey green shirt.

Hey, what the fuck? Oh, I see. It's a gun. Playing cowgirls and Indians out here? I know it's a lot of fun, but it's damn hot out here. The last wild Indians left Georgia a hundred years ago anyway. Come on, Bonnie. Give me the stick.

She backed away.

He smiled, holding out his hand.

Hey, come with me now and you can come back out here in the morning. What d'ya say? Come on. Don't give me a hassle.

Bonnie waited. She backed up further.

Girl, you want to keep your yard privileges, you better come on now.

Trapped, she dropped her rifle.

It's no good anyhow. If I kill him out in the open like this, they'll know who did it and I won't have a chance. Shit.

She turned and ran.

The whistle blew behind her. Three more puke green shirts emerged from the trees and spread out in front of her.

Damn. I gotta let 'em catch me. I'll pretend I was confused again. Then maybe they won't squeeze my arms so hard or choke me, like usual.

Oral purification

When Carla opened the dentist's office door, chilled air scented with peppermint and cloves rushed out.

A spicy fog rose up to her knees before she quickly stepped inside and slammed the door and fell into the arms of the leggy hygienist who just happened to be waiting with a floor-length ermine coat trimmed with a collar of albino and black foxtails. Even though Carla clung to her vegan and animal right's activism tighter than her navel ring pinched her button belly, she couldn't help squirming and cooing "Oooooo" as she slid her fingers up and down, twining them in and out of the fur.

The hygienist held up a long mirror and the secretary and the two assistant hygienists gathered around to admire Carla in the coat. With her ebony hair and skin the color of roasted peanuts, if she'd screeched and waved her arms, nobody would have objected: dentists' offices need shamans as much as TV studios do.

In fact, at that moment, from beyond the mirror and walls, a piercing howling erupted as if a pack of small hunting dogs was getting closer.

Carla, naturally alert and by training super-sensitized, tried to wiggle out of the coat, but the foxtails had formed a knot, the in-and-out-of-the-rabbit hole kind that only an experienced sailor can untie.

Dr. Kuzukawa slinked out of his operating parlor, pumping a breath freshening mister between thin lips, and griped, "Ladies. Did you forget you had three patients on nitrogen?" He smiled at Carla, whose face had gone beet, and said, "Are you my two o'clock root canal?"

"Just a cleaning," she whispered.

The foxtails scented the rabbit and closed in and Carla began to stutter and lose her breath until the gallant Dr. K loosened the collar, slipped the coat off her shoulders, and dropped it in the hygienist's hands.

"OK, Betty, you can turn the heat up now," Dr K said, turning away, "but not over sixty two. Can't have the drills overheating, can we?"

If I were Carla, I'd get out of that crazy office as fast as I could, but not our girl. Dr. K gave the spiffiest, whitest cleaning in town, and she had a date that night with someone who might, well, the odds were finally stacking up in her favor, someone who might be The One. He was vegan, had money, cute as anybody she'd dated, and had asked her to dinner three times before she said yes.

She ran her tongue over her teeth, ready for her annual oral purification.

Drums call from the distance

Having shifted his emotional Range Rover into neutral, he let the island winds blow through the open windows of his mind.

How else could he bear the grind of sitting at a desk typing someone else's lies that nobody but he knew were lies? He knew because the wind spoke in sub-audible syllables, reminding him of the drums hammering and the great pillar of burning trees the dead king had planted thirty years ago and cut down and dried, saving them for today's sacrifice of lions and gazelles.

The original markets existed for women buying and selling produce and for crippled men to make a living off the tools they constructed, for children playing underfoot and for young people to meet before marriage. Today every place you go you find yourself in the middle of a market. All you have to do is turn on your TV or radio. Most people spend their days responding to advertising and making whoever runs the market rich. Who needed money? he thought. The old king spit on money.

"Go and be there," he mumbled to himself. "Go and be there."

He repeated the last words he'd typed for next week's travel ad: "Imagine. You're where you belong. Your dreams have come true. Now, why don't you just go and be there." He noticed the final phrase he was supposed to type: "You use your mind to make up your ideal place. We'll fly you there before you know it."

"Now or never," he said out loud.

The Range Rover began to rumble and rattle. He rolled up the windows, snapped his seat belt tight, shifted into first, stood up and feeling the drumbeats vibrate in his heels, he walked out the office door toward the howling flames his laughing brothers fed with copier paper and neckties and office clothes. The burning shoes stunk, and the blinding sun and the pounding drums in his head and the heat crackling on his cheeks and the smell of sizzling meat made him dizzy.

He switched on the Rover's air conditioning. As soon as the air cooled, his head cleared. Smiling, he pulled out of the office parking lot, bounced down the rutted trail, letting the drums boil in his chest. He stepped on it, spewing dust clouds behind. He wondered if he had enough gas to last him until the next watering hole. Just in case, he'd stop for a fill and a six-pack at the 7-11.

And then he was gone.

Goal-getting workshop

"What is a goal?" he asked, his mouth brimming with secret powers the class craved.

"Something you want?" the lawyer volunteered.

"A problem to solve," the accountant piped up.

"Mmm hmm." Their teacher, narrow-eyed and pugnacious, said, "Do any of you have a goal?"

"A fortune teller told me his name twenty years ago. We exchange emails every day. I really want to marry him-that's my goal." The attractive brunette with the vertical furrow between her eyebrows leaned back in her folding chair, exhausted from her self-revelation to two dozen strangers.

"That's a goal," the teacher confirmed, nodding.

The woman sat up. "I came here hoping you could fix it so we'd get married."

Tossing chalk up and down, everyone in the class focused on its path, the teacher said, "What am I supposed to fix? Is there a problem?"

You could sense the set-up in the teacher's mind: a desire and an obstruction: the stuff every lesson is made of.

"A little one. Sort of."

"Tell us," a few women in the class encouraged. "Maybe we can help."

The woman shifted on the chair and propped her elbows on the table, then confessed, "He's married."

"What?" the teacher said, fumbling with his chalk.

"He's married," echoed from three or four attentive class members.

"Oh," the teacher said, kneeling down to retrieve his chalk, "that is a problem." He turned away from the goal-seeking solution-needing woman and faced the class. "It's a goal, too. A big goal."

"A big goal," fifteen voices chimed.

"OK, let's everybody think it over," the teacher said. "We'll brainstorm when we come back from break."

Every class member but one returned from break early, the merciful eager to point out the obvious pitfalls, the righteous ready to conceal their condemnations in questions like, "Does he have kids? How do you know you love each other?" and the numbly curious who found themselves in a mild form of Reality TV. The only class member who skipped out at break was the woman with the problem.

The ex- accountant asked the teacher, "Was she one of your friends? Did you set that up?"

The teacher's eyes bulged and his jaw fell and he splayed his arms wide, palms out.

No one spoke until one of the women said, "I'll kill you if you fix that. Think of the kids."

A ruddy man wearing a black and ripped Harley Davidson t-shirt piped up, "Hey, man, don't make a judgment. We don't know the whole story."

A murmur of agreement ran through half the class. The other half smirked, got up and left, talking in loud, recriminating voices.

The Tibetan

"Why so glum?" Juanita Bloom asked her breakfast regular, Herman Wazclewski. She lay his plate – the usual: two golden eyes with suntanned Irishmen, pacifist – beside his knife and spoon.

He stared at the eggs and dipped his fork into the greasy spuds and stirred, mumbling into his chin, "It's my last life," he said. "I stole and lied and cheated. I was so rich I owned two mansions."

"That last part's not bad," the scrawny waitress said, aching for a cigarette. "Let me order you some toast. Nice blueberry jam'll make you feel better." She turned and hollered, "Double soldier," then filled Herman's cup with hot chocolate.

Herman sipped. "You had a last life as a saint," he said, "but I was a slimy crook. Now I'm broke, no love, and I get up to pee five times a night."

She took away his untouched plate. It was pheasant hunting season and men in red and black plaid coats and hats stood in line, waiting for a place to sit and devour nets drenched in druid's blood. She gave Herman another try. "Want waffles instead? Mmmm." She smacked her lips. "Hot maple syrup."

He pursed his lips.

Juanita had to move the traffic, so she said, "Go over to the Tibetans. They'll fix you up. Make you a beggar or a prisoner in your past life. Wipe all the sin out of you."

"Who's The Tibetans?"

"You know, it's those bald guys who wear orange robes and red scarves. Live in Matt Wilson's place on Seventh." Just then, Juanita looked up to see her brother, Nick, waltzing in, expecting a free cuppa joe, no doubt. Juanita thought he looked quite striking today in his new quilted saffron-colored hunting jacket with a maroon cap bent casually over his shiny head, his shotgun slung butt-up across his shoulder. "Yo, Nick," she hollered above the breakfast din and hunters' hubbub, "no guns at the counter." An older sister always had to tell the young one how to behave in public.

Herman's eyes trailed her voice across the diner and landed on Nick who was dressed like a sunrise and dutifully leaning his .20 guage Winchester against the pea-green wall. He must be one of those Tibetans. The past life criminal got up to go sit beside him. If he can't fix my last life, maybe he can arrange something nice for my next one.

Juanita sponged off the counter and said to her next regular, "What can I do you for, Mister Scott?"

"The usual," Mr. Scott said, pulling out his flask and pouring an amber finger into his coffee cup. "And a latte chaser."

Fifteen, forlorn, freaked

Like, would I climb into his Cherokee if I didn't expect to give them both blow jobs? I'm not stupid. What do think it means when boys ask you to go for a ride? Yeah, I told them both they could fuck, but they wouldn't. I knew they wouldn't do a fifteen year old. I'm like you, you know. I say things to freak people out. So don't you freak on me.

You know what else? I'd bring them home and let them do whatever they felt like if you weren't home. Drink everything in your cabinet. That's what I told them at the mall. Only I didn't know whose house to go to so we drove by mom's cuz she's never home on Saturday night but her Camry was sitting outside, like she didn't go yet or something. No way I'm taking my friends inside if she's there. She'd freak. She freaks at everything. She freaked at my lizard tattoo. She freaked at my biology teacher. So we came over here, but you were home, too.

You were probably upstairs fuckin that bimbo Jeannie again, like if you could think of anything else. Like she's what? Twenty-six?

The princess's embroidery and the bonobos

While prince charming sleeps, the princess rides home thru the darkness.

At one point, she realizes that she is sleepy too, so she pulls over and asks her unconscious mind to take the wheel & wake her up when she is home.

When sparkling light danced on her eyelids in the morning, she felt kissed by the sun. lolling under warm blankets in her cool bedroom, the princess wondered if she stayed in bed, would the prince arrive or would she just drift off into dreams, while another busy day of the harvest season escaped her.

She drowsed, not really having made up her mind but she did understand, before falling back to sleep, that she'd rather let the daylight capture her than find day captive in her hands.

Later, when the prince arrived, she had already finished weaving the left shoulder of her first silver and emerald-plaited finely spun ivory mantle.

She planned to embroider on it with gold thread a magical scene all across the body of the robe: people doing everything, animals profound and numerous, birds, insects, fish, flowers, trees, fields, skies with sun and stars and clouds, in fact, the whole world revealing its true soul, as she saw it, shimmering in beauty, offering joy.

Each mantle had a place and a purpose, some she wore less now than others, but all mantles deserved the honor of adorning her. If she wore this mantle everywhere, she couldn't be happier. She had other robes, some daily leather, some spring and summer ceremonial linen, thick red wool for winter, delicate silk for summer nights' dancing

Among those hanging in her wardrobe, the princess rarely chose from one corner. When she did reach into the shadowy end of the closet, she never failed to choose a gorgeous robe, a robe that elevated her status in her eyes and the eyes of others to the rank of bearer of true witness. Yet the burden of such a robe - the ebony and gold velvet riding mantle whose colors caused her to disappear, or the soft albino ermine and pale Chinese silk whose pride reduced her kingdom to a region where the people suffered because of the floods and she must maintain daily watch for storms in the high valleys, or the audacity of the double-weave yellow silk robe of royal longing for immortality she wore with mahogany leather gloves as if she herself deserved the love of all.

She put aside her work and rose from her table when she heard the prince's car rumble into her courtyard. She picked up a peach and nibbled it while she sauntered to the outer door of her cottage to watch him climb out. His smile pleased her so much she decided that she'd embroider it into the face of the male chimpanzee she'd been working on.

Later, when she told him her intention, he laughed

and said, hey, it's a bonobo smile all the way. And you know what bonobos like to do a lot and do a lot?

Of course, the princess knew about bonobos. She blushed. Thank goodness, only a prince dared speak to a princess like that.

Salt substitute

Horrified by the maggots slithering around the wound on his leg, the church lady peeled back the papery trousers from the legs dangling from the wheelchair in front of the library and plucked the odious bugs, dropping them one by one on onto the sidewalk.

The old paraplegic's pal stomped on them, pirouetting as he slimed the cement with their bodies.

I didn't mind them, the old boy in the chair said. Couldn't feel 'em, really.

Everybody got somethin like this, his friend said. With me, it's women. Hey, he shouted to the passers-by, anybody got some salt?

The church lady gulped, revolted and saddened to her toes that the men might have to eat the squashed maggots.

The man noticed her clenching her stomach. Hey, he said, the sidewalk's slippery. All greasy. Just wanna salt it down so nobody falls on his ass. He laughed.

The church lady happened to have a portable jar of salt substitute in her bag. Food these days tasted so bland, but her blood pressure ... she placed it in the man's hand.

He bowed to her and unscrewed the cap and poured, writing "Jim" in salt substitute on the maggot remains.

Roosters

At five oh three this morning I turned cutthroat.

Those damned roosters next door crowbarred into my dreams like kickboxers flailing my dream body and shredding it into a tatter of fading memories.

I wanted to throttle them the way wattle-armed Mrs. Stackowicz does back in Deerfield, and I saw myself slitting their throats like Gawain decapitated the Green Knight fifteen hundred years ago,

Then my nice self thought, if I succeed with my rooster pogrom, what would Isabel and Hank do for hen inseminators? They need to sell eggs to afford their kids' schools and even rooster-loving eggs farmers deserve vacations now and then.

I realized this because the first principle of my psychotherapeutic practice is empathy as a goal and as a technique.

After breakfast, I discussed the problem with Annette, who lives next door, on the other side from the roosters. She cited the appropriate and clandestine application of the somewhat unprincipled shotgun technique.

"I don't give a fig about empathy," she said. "Everybody's got empathy. Action. That's what matters. Action."

I agreed a shotgun would work, but would it solve my problem of empathy for Hank and Isabel? I didn't buy the action thing. Perhaps I should try to like the taste of eggs instead of genociding their source. I just don't know if I can get over the sulfury taste of the yolks. Even if I could, I'll never be able to bear that runny feeling on my tongue.

"It's yolks or the shotgun," Annette the action girl apprised.

Now I don't know what to do. I'll try to sleep on it, but I doubt if I can.

The nose knows

Ramona came home from work about as excited as I'd ever seen her in the afternoon. She dropped her reticule purse on the couch and plucked a gardenia from behind her ear.

"Smell this," she said.

I put down the TV remote and leaned over, placing my nose close to the heart of the flower. One sniff and I was back on our first date ... or was it our first kiss? No, it was the time her cousin Harun introduced us. Yes, that was it.

I'd stopped by the greenhouse where my friend Harun worked to collect the fifty dollars he owed me. I needed it in those days when the prices were climbing to record heights. A woman was there with Harun, tossing gardenia petals around. As they floated down, she ran under them, laughing.

Harun was scowling when he introduced us. Waving his arm at her, his sour face an apology for her silliness in the middle of the serious business of growing flowers. "My cousin, Ramona," he growled.

Back in the present, I looked up at her, my nose still in the flower. "This is delicious," I said, sniffing.

"I quit my job," Ramona said. "Mr. Calhoun's constant niceness finally got to me."

Slightly shocked, I said, "Didn't you read the survey? 87% of Americans say their bosses are dictators. You were lucky."

Ramona twiddled the gardenia in her fingers. "He was the dictator of collaboration," she said. "He always asked my opinion about anything before he did it. If I so much as raised an eyebrow, he backed off."

She was caressing my cheek with the flower, dragging it across my lips. This time I definitely remembered our first date at the Japanese tea garden sipping tea and sniffing flowers.

I mumbled, "Sounds like you were the real boss."

"Not really. Besides, I like a little authority and know-it-all-ness sometimes. I can't take a man who doesn't follow his own mind." Her eyes sparkled.

I stood up and grabbed her wrist. "I don't care what you think," I said, gripping firmly. "You're coming with me."

I tugged her toward the bedroom, caring not a whit that without her job we'd lose our health insurance. Being married to an old-fashioned girl makes a man a happy man. I learned from the Morning Show just that day that happiness is the main factor behind staying healthy. And plenty of sex, they said. I believe it. I haven't had a cold in years.

Polo, curling, and, ...?

Bill Sampson drove a pretty nice car, not what he wanted or could afford, but he was saving for a horse. Bill loved polo. He'd never played on a team, but he'd practiced on his own and with other amateurs for the last three years.

A few months back, Bill had a good shot at joining one of the West's better polo teams, right at the club where he rode. Unfortunately, the spot the team invited him to fill was vacated by a former member who fell off his horse and broke his neck while swatting a routine ball.

Bill was not superstitious, since his childhood on the potato farm in Maine, but he'd always known which way the wind blew. In Maine, it blew from the north and east. In California, it blew from the west and the north. So, he declined the invitation, saving himself the hefty team fees while waiting another year or two when some old duffer would retire and pass on a safe, warm saddle.

In any case, Bill had his eye on a young Morgan he could ride in competition for years, once they got used to each other. Not only that, a sloe-eyed Jamaican woman who worked at the same bank he worked at smiled at him every time they saw each other.

"Things look good," he told his mother. "I want a nicer car and a team membership, but I'm adapting to my circumstances. This girl at the bank is pretty and in Jamaica, polo is common as whatever they call that game with bowlers and batters. Not curling."

"Cricket," she said.

"That's it. Thanks, mom. You'd win Jeopardy every time. But the thing I love about you, when I can't have what I want, I adapt. You raised me to adapt."

"Adapt? Adapt? I raised you to set a goal and go for it. Nothing gets in your way."

"Sure, sure. My goal right now is another piece of that rhubarb crumble. How about it?"

His mother pushed the whole dish across the table, continuing her son's behavior modification. A mom's work is never done. She wanted to see a picture of the girl and hear about her family before she helped Sam adapt to her, or not.

The soul mate's sluice

She positioned herself behind the ficus tree to observe the dancers in the sunken ballroom below, obscuring herself from Oscar. I knew this because, as her soul mate, I grasped her every motive. Her thinking was far more complicated than mine. My gift commands great reservoirs of tears that I offer to her any time I sense she needs them, expecting rejection and usually receiving it with a sweet kiss on my nose or a tousle through my thinning hair when her fingers feel like those haboops or mistrals swarming in from the south.

Peeking between the branches, she watched the dancers, tapping her toes, chewing her cheek. Eventually Oscar glanced up as he spun Roberta in an elegant figure eight double helix twirl. Roberta's blue and gold crinoline skirt flared out and brushed Oscar's knees, just the instant his eyes met my soul mate's. He smiled and she turned her back on him, her face to me.

"Open the sluice a little, Rami," she said. "I don't wanna cry me a river, but I need a good spring stream."

I leaned into the wheel that turned the valves to raise the plate holding the tears back. The screw was rusted but it gave in to my strength and pretty soon, a trickle began to leak down the spillway. I told her to relax and let it flow. She couldn't handle the volume I could, or you could, so I took it easy on the valves. She braced herself against the ficus and let the tears fall onto the cracked earth in the pot until they filled it and began to overflow.

"That's enough, Rami. Don't want to drown the tree, now, do we?"

I cranked the barrier plate almost all the closed, leaving a thread of tears seeping down, in case she needed them later.

The vocation

He came late to his trade of magic.

At least, he thought so until he remembered he'd never once felt satisfied with his life, how it caromed through a troubling world, heart-breaking and beautiful as it was. He bamboozled nobody except himself, most likely because he was bored by cards, took little pleasure in showboating, had shaky hands and a mind too restless to bear pitching knives for hours in a dusty tent. Worse, he'd lost the twin souls of magic, belief and falsehood.

In his never-ending training, he'd spent decades sleepwalking in a wizard hat and shimmery silk pajamas, making his way among the tumult of people, eventually learning to hear the their sub-lingual self-talk, the source of the magician's appeal. Often, he heard, "Am I good enough?" "Will you still love me once you get to know me?" "Keep your distance, fool!"

Still, all he knew was to stroll along with everyone, listening to their thought-whistles, as they walked down the dim yet sun-splashed path to the graveyard just beyond the gardens and orchards.

Stopping beside the trail, under the shade of an oak whose leaves fluttered like nervous spirits, the man saw the battle each person must enter: A game, played with the stakes of a clash between kingdoms, whose victory exalted the winners only if they accepted with their ascendant wings an endless course of sadness winding through their hearts.

He pulled an old notebook from his pocket, leaned against the tree, and read his last entry, "Fire makes ash. Ash rises on the wind, makes clouds and brings down rain. Rain wakes the seeds." Raising his eyes to the blue sky and nodding to the clouds, he grasped his life's work – installing lightning rods in souls, grounding them in bones, blood, and flesh.

Three wise men

Three of the wisest men of the early twenty first century met at Freddies Old Fashioneds & Coffee Shop.

After shaking hands and muttering the usual, "Nice to see you again. How's the wife?"

"You lose some weight?"

They sat down to drink spiked java and get to work. Being wise, first they twinkled all around, observing meaning in every wrinkle and sip in the room.

The youngest, from Sri Lanka, garbed in a royal blue sarong and always carrying a pocketful of vegetable samosas, said, quoting himself, "Be strong like a coconut, but don't go crazy, Coco Lopez."

His companions giggled at this loony cosmic jest.

The wisest of the three, a Frenchman down from Quebec, proposed a toast. "To the question!"

They raised their ceramic mugs in silence, beaming and pink-lipped as Freddies' neon OPEN sign.

Then, the other man, the neo-Zen Japanese voted most recently into the inner sanctum of the world's wisest, felt a caffeine rush and, figuring action was needed, scooted out of the booth. Just before he pushed open the restroom door, he turned and shouted to his wise men's group, "Unify for peace!"

At that, Hector and Nikolai, the town's senior garbage men taking their break at the counter, slapped their wallets to make sure they had their ID's and hollered back, in unison,

"Love is all you need."

At that, the Sri Lankan and the Frenchman smashed their mugs into a plumb white shards on the floor and bulled out of the joint leaving the bill and the tip for their decidedly drunk Japanese pal.

The two wise men stood outside lighting up so-called non-carcinogenic Players cigarettes and puffed clouds of smoke into autumn sunshine.

Back at the counter, Hector said to his buddy, "Like we said."

"Love bugs, that's us," Nikolai agreed. "Hey, Meg," he called to Freddie's thick-ankled wife who nevertheless wore three-inch patent leather Prada heels to work every day.

"Refills here?"

She poured the coffee. "How's that, boys?

"Perfect," Hector said. "Dasvadanya."

"Hugalug"

Somebody stopped right there in the middle of the road, sixty steep feet up a steep bushy bank from the river, for no good reason.

Jessica braked. The car just sat there, idling. She waited, oh, thirty seconds, time enough to light a cigarette, roll down her window, blow out the smoke while she looked down into the silvery water foaming over boulders.

She loved the taste of the first of the day. Observed with pleasure herself lighting up. She had nothing better to do for just a few seconds, not long enough to actually think about anything, until she became conscious of the smoke in her eyes and the rush in her chest and throat aching and fingers almost tingling.

Not that she was in a hurry, if she was, she wouldn't be way out here in the middle of nowhere cruising around like a wandering puppy, but the forward motion of driving nagging in her muscles needed translation out of brake mode, into some action, some doing other than strumming her fingers on the steering wheel or changing stations or CD's. That's it. She decided to play the new SponTaNeo Josh gave her.

The car ahead sat as still as when she nearly crashed into it a moment ago, so she rummaged through the layer of CD's and papers on the passenger seat and found the SponTaNeo "Hugalug" album.

An odd drab cover on it – metallic rainbow overhead, iridescent violet sea with white caps in background, and up close, on a boat, a profile of the naked trunks of three or was it four? people, grappling with each other.

She examined it, twisted it around. From one angle, the four looked like the face of a bloodhound, its wrinkles folded in on each other. From another, she saw a man and a woman kissing across the back of a turtle, or was it a deck of cards? Anyway, who cared? She wasn't even sure she liked hiphop, but Josh told her she had to listen – he never heard anything so cool.

A cold mist crept up the riverbank, its curious tendrils curling toward the cars. In her rear view mirror, she saw her Rav 4's thick exhaust funnel upward across and up the rear window.

Glancing forward, she noticed the stopped car had turned off its engine. It had no exhaust cloud.

I wonder … they OK? she thought.

Inserting the new CD, she leaned over the steering wheel and peered into the car ahead. She didn't see anyone in the driver's seat or anywhere in the car.

Maybe the driver had gotten out to look at the view over the oxbow–amazing how wide the river was right there, curving around like somebody writing an endless word filled with s's and i's. A message written by the earth.

SponTaNeo's first drum beats punched into her ears as she strained to see.

Jessica knew everything had a meaning to it, if you could just get it. Trouble was, the way the hills and the sky and the towns all melted together, they covered up the writings and signs. Sometimes, like maybe now, you get a glimpse of something and you know, if you could only read it, your life would change in some way, some small but real way.

She opened her car door and put one foot on the ground. She had to make sure the people were OK, or ask them to pull over a little. The road would be wide enough for her to pass if they tucked their car tight against the bluff.

She definitely wouldn't risk trying to go around them – the hill poured straight down to the valley floor. She had to ask them to move over. She was a good driver, because she didn't take stupid risks.

Violins came up over SponTaNeo's throbbing percussion, rising like a fragrant wind pouring out of her speakers. That's odd, she thought, wanting to listen further before she got out of the car. I never heard strings like that. Then a man's sultry voice unfurled a low groan as if he were lifting something immensely heavy, and then the singer began to hum a kind of da da bu ba ba scat until it broke into a soft laugh, the way Josh bubbled up when she tickled him, low, welcoming, his chuckling teasing her to tickle harder and make him laugh and wiggle until he grabbed her arms.

The seductive violins segued into muted clarinets and sotto trombones setting up the sultry voice again. SponTaNeo moaned a slow gospel chant, "You gonna do it...with me create...now, baby ...Honeydew, don't be makin...me wait... you know who's...captain ... your fate... my boots...openin up... the gate ...." Bass drums thudded, vibrating through her seat.

Yeah, he was good, like Josh said, worth hearing, but

not the coolest ever. She'd listen to it while she watched the car up there for one more minute.

She turned up the volume and stepped out with both feet. In her heels she had to pick her way between stones on the gravel road. She wished she'd brought sneakers with her. Broad shouldered now, and insistent, cool river air climbed out of the valley and hoisted itself over the edge of the unrailed embankment.

Shivering, Jessica reminded herself to do some deep breathing. Inhaling and exhaling moist flooding air always relaxed her more than anything, and warmed her up.

She approached the car, a wide, low older car, dirty amber with a matching row of rust spots where a strip of chrome used to be. A low beat, nearly the same beat she'd left playing in her car, fell out of the open windows and seeped across the road, roiling bright shapes and subtle greens and maroons into the mist.

The beat caressing her bare calves.

The stopped car was only a few feet away. It was shimmying on its wheels. The old car swaying in tune with the music? It couldn't be. The wind blowing against it? River breeze barely stirred the mist.

"Hello," she said, bending forward from her waist, ducking her head to mid-window. "Hello?"

She stayed back from the car door, peering into the wing mirror, not wanting to upset anybody. She was sorry she had to interrupt them, but she couldn't wait around till they finished. It was too embarrassing, and none of her business, even if it was really kind of wild to come on people doing it in a car in the middle of the day. She could never see herself like that, but she admired people who felt so free.

This time she spoke louder. "Hello. Anybody there."

A man's head popped up from the back seat and, in the shadow on the far side of the interior, turned to look at her. He said something, but not to her, and another head appeared, staring at Jessica over the man's shoulder. He hefted his body around – she could see he was wearing a shirt – and the woman sat up. In the background, Jessica heard SponTaNeo's sexy voice crooning "...wait...mate...date...extrapolate...." What was that word? She had to listen closer, when she got back to her car.

The man leaned his head out the window, a huge grin smeared across his face. He was bald with white sideburns and his cheeks flamed and shiny. Jessica thought she hadn't seen such a happy face since who knows? Forever. The man reminded her of her father, who she never saw so happy. The man laughed a deep belly laugh and his girlfriend started laughing, too. Jessica smiled and chuckled a little. It was pretty funny.

"Sorry, young lady," the man said. "I see we're blockin the road. Just such a beautiful day...my wife and I...we come here when we can...four kids...grand kids...you know, gets kinda crowded at home...you're the first one's ever come up on us...."

"Sorry." Jessica said, the word barely emerging from her throat. Then, "Sir."

He laughed again. "I ain't no sir, that's for sure."

Their eyes focused on each other, he with sparkling blue eyes, she staring and smiling, her cheeks loosening a little more the longer his cheery eyes invited her to say more.

"Umm," she said, "umm, could you, uh, move your car?"

He laughed again, as if he'd never enjoyed himself more. "Sure. Kinda tight up here, ain't it?" His pudgy wife giggled and slapped him on the back. "Gimme a minute," he said.

"Thanks," she said, and began to back away toward her car, then stopped. "You know what's really weird? I mean, not you. What it is, we're both playing the same CD – 'Hugalug'."

"That right? He's fine. But you be careful, listening to him, driving your car, all by yourself. Could be a fit comes over you and you get in a wreck." He laughed and his wife slapped him again, percussing him with both hands on his shoulders this time. The woman's blueberry dark eyes settled on Jessica's, then blinked, then she smiled, they smiled at each other.

Jessica said, "Thanks, I'll watch out." She turned back to her car. SponTaNeo's voice urged her to climb into her warm front seat, wait for the old dude to move.

She thought she heard "Jesse, don't run off and make a messa me, I got the only thing you ever gonna needa see." The horns dropped to a low pitch and muffled the words, but not the intention.

As she turned to slide sideways into her car, she looked up and saw the man tumbling over into his front seat. He wasn't fat and she couldn't tell is he had his pants on or not. His wife sat in back, twisted around, looking back at her. The woman waved and Jesse waved back.

The old car started and vile exhaust fumes drifted in Jesse's window. She rolled it up and exhaled as fully as she could. She covered her nose with her mouth and inhaled into her gut, put her car in gear, and resumed her riverside drive. She edged past the couple in the old car and turned to wave good-bye. They'd turned up the sound of their CD player and SponTaNeo's voice rumbled, the horns howled, and the drums thumped the air so hard, Jesse felt her car shake. Rocking their shoulders and nodding their heads, the old lovers grinned and waved.

Once past them, she looked in her rear view mirror but the mist had thickened and she lost sight of the old car parked beyond the curve of the bluff.

Blood Medicine

A silver Mercedes waited in front of the hotel. Woo told me to lie across the back seat, "to rest your back," while he rode in front with Lin, the driver. The stout car rolled along the pitted streets as gently as a raft floating across a still pond. The neoned night flowed across the oily windows in synthetic rainbow colors. As we wound through the streets toward Old Taipei, I lay drowsing, sunk in leather cushions, relaxed and content.

We stopped abruptly and Woo said over his shoulder, sharply, "Goddam politicians. Let's go, Charlie. We have to walk. Lin will watch the car."

Angry shouts punctuated by firecrackers popping roared into the car as Woo opened the door. People ran by waving flags and banging on trash can lids.

"It's the government. The new generation thinks it's their turn now. The old boys want to show they still get hard-ons."

"We have demonstrations in the States all the time," I said.

He gripped my arm and led me against the current of the crowd. My sense of being a pawn in someone else's game sharpened, but all I could do was play along. I might as well enjoy myself.

We crossed into an open loading lot where dozens of reeking dumpsters lined the walls on four sides of the square. A throng of men milled around in the putrid night, shouting at each other, hip-checking boxes onto pallets, pirouetting out of the way of the smut-blatting motor scooters, all at an earnest commercial pitch. My nostrils twinged as exhaust fumes assaulted my face.

"Trash sorters," Woo said, impervious to the stinking vapors. "When the shops close, they pick through the dumpsters. They sell to Beijing. Very rich men."

A wave of fatigue rolled over me. My watch said midnight. How long had I dozed in the back of the car? I wanted to go back to the hotel and sleep away my growing befuddlement. The scotch had worn off and the pain had climbed from an ache in my lower back to a knife under my shoulder blades.

Taiwan had taken my measure and I was a lot smaller here than I'd ever been back home and I felt no need to prove myself any more. For a moment, I shocked myself with a stroke of longing to be back in Clem, volleying with the Chief, worrying about sales, dealing with all the routine problems that made my mundane life exciting. Taipei had satisfied my appetite for the exotic and now I was ready to bring the taste of it to America and spread my epiphany of Soy to the World.

I slowed down to watch the trash sorters, night buzzards their riches from deals with government agents, no doubt. Several thin men scrambled in and out of the dumpsters, hollering at each other. An ebony Hummer sat sentry in the shadows at the end of the block.

Woo picked up his pace, tugging my arm hard and drawing me out of my half-soused reverie. We turned the corner and entered into a chartreuse beam glowing from the wall of a building. We stepped through an open storefront into a wide, high-ceilinged shop lit by shining neon ideographs. Glistening white tiles rose to meet wall-length mirrors reflecting so much light that most of the dozen of so people in the room wore sunglasses.

I followed Woo to the back of the shop, my leather soles clicking over the terracotta floor tiles. The shop smelled slightly of rancid fat or old meat, reminding me of a large restaurant kitchen or the butchery in a grocery store. It was set with trestle tables.

I pointed to the many eight-inch long geckos that perched near the corner between the walls and ceiling. Woo said, "Geckos. Do you see any flies?"

I shook my head no.

"Geckos," he said, dismissing further gecko small talk.

Seven or eight boisterous men and a few animated women sat at the table talking. A thin bald man called out "New York!" and raised his glass and toasted me. He tossed off his deep purple wine quickly, leapt up on a chair and began chanting at me, pointing to himself, to his image in the wall mirror, and then back to me.

Watching him over my shoulder, I closed the distance between Woo and myself, hoping to defuse the drunk by ignoring him. Woo stopped short and I bumped into him. Groaned an apology for my clumsiness.

"Don't pay attention to him," Woo said, dismissing my self-reproach. "There, Big Man's coming to throw him out."

The largest man I'd seen in Taiwan strolled across the room. Standing at least seven feet tall and four feet wide, his wore an ivory cotton business suit, white shirt, and black headband restraining a shock of silver hair on his basketball-size head.

The giant curled a trunk of an arm around the drunk's neck and lifted him up, then dangling him at arm's length. The surprised man twitched on the bouncer's hip, gasping and grunting and kicking as the other drinkers laughed at his predicament.

Oblivious to the commotion, Woo stared intently into a large rectangular aquarium from which, I guessed, he'd select a fish for our midnight dinner. I'd had seafood every dinner since we arrived in Taipei and each dish was exquisitely different from the next.

I edged around Woo to stand beside him, watching him as he made up his mind. The aquarium windows were dry and I couldn't see any fish. The tank's shadowy floor gleamed in the room's haze, an emerald and ivory sheen pulsing slowly, sloshing, like brackish water. A sweet, pungent odor wafted out of the tank.

As Woo stared into the aquarium, I raised my eyes to

toward the room. Hundreds of shadowy, flayed snake skins were attached to the wall behind the tank, some entwined, some laid over others, the longest of them climbing from floor to dusky ceiling and stretching out over the room, a bas relief of flat scaly vines. The widest and longest pelts hung like woven blankets, died in earthen tans and browns, patterned in diamonds and swirls, artfully connected with repeated crosshatches.

I stared into the tank: the "fish" in it were living, coiling snakes. The sluggish water reflections were snakes oozing over and under each other, warming themselves in the friction of muscle on silken muscle. A field of lidless eyes sparkled. Blunt heads rose and dipped, curved and turned, pausing in the air as if curious, as if sensing us through the slashes in the sides of their noses. Flattened ping pong ball heads probing algae-green turkey eggs Warming each other with friction.

A short man wearing an orange and blue flowered shirt draped over an ample stomach approached, smiling, speaking rapidly as he waved his arm over the tank. He reached in, brushing aside several nodding heads. He rummaged through the writhing mound like someone sorting laundry.

Woo barked at the man as he lifted a snake, dangling it in front of my face while letting it's tail brush back and forth on the floor. Afraid I'd blunder, I braced myself, waiting for a clue from Woo.

The man quickly tossed the snake back and bowed to Woo, glancing sideways at me. He signaled for us to follow him. We passed a large cage holding four small monkeys. I stopped Woo to ask about them.

"What are these little guys doing here?"

He was so intent on following the tropical shirt, he didn't understand what I meant, so I pointed.

"Oh, the monkeys. They love snake. They clean up afterwards. Every year, Big Man brings in the animal of the year. You should see it when it's Tiger year." He laughed. "He puts a baby tiger inside and all the women in the mall want to come in to pet it. Our best year for business."

"What does he do for a dragon," I asked, challenging him with a grin.

He laughed and said, "Come back and see."

I might just do that. Maybe I should imitate that idea in my office. On second thought, my office staff would resign if I had a bunch of monkeys or dogs, of God forbid, rats in cages in my office. I'd have to make due with photos or little statues in Clem. Every year, I'd give our customers a Year of the Whatever Animal promotional statue working toward a complete set of twelve animals, each subtly, tastefully engraved with our logo.

Close behind Woo, I pushed through clacking bamboo strips hung across a doorway into a room about the size of my office back in Clem. Behind the far wall, which was glass from floor to ceiling, was a forest scene: thick, smooth tree trunks, broad leaves, ferns, moisture trails trickling down inside the glass.

The man disappeared while Woo and I sat down in thickly upholstered chairs across the room from the jungle diorama.

"Relax, Charlie," Woo said. His face shadowed in the dim light seeping out of the aquarium into the room. He sat lightly in his chair, leaning forward almost eagerly.

"What's going on, Woo?"

"Our lucky night, Charlie. Mr. Meng said spare no expense. Huan went to get us the finest snake in the house."

Huan and another man emerged from the doorway beside the aquarium. Huan backed into the room, bracing him self against the floor, pulling the tongue of a long wooden wagon with three foot high sides and wide rubber wheels. The other man bent over behind the wagon, his arms locked straight, palms against the rear wall, straining to push the cart ahead. Water, or some mysterious fluid, dripped from the cart's seams.

Grinning at the snake handler, Woo bounced up from his chair, and I followed him over to the cart. Inside, a huge snake lay tangled, embracing itself, bulging against the side walls, bowing the thin planks. A shudder of its mass and the wagon walls would shatter.

The snake's body was the color of a faded red barn tattooed with rows of brown footballs. A large black and tan cantaloupe with open, still, silver eyes laying passively on top of the glittering mound of its body.

I'd never seen anything like it. "God, where did they get that thing?"

"They raised it. From an egg. Takes years."

"What is it? I've never heard of a snake this big."

"Anaconda. Lives in the water and eats deer and wild pigs."

The men tugged and pushed the cart toward the store's front room. Huan snapped something to the man in the rear and Woo laughed. "Stay back, Charlie. Don't get too close to the head. It'll grab and wind itself around your neck."

I jumped back. Shades of my worst nightmare as a kid - I'm strolling along a shady sidewalk and a snake drops out of a tree and strangles me to death. As soon as I spooked, the three Chinese burst into belly laughs. More cultural confusion. As long as my Chinese associates found me funny and laughed, I didn't mind. That showed their pleasure in my company, even if in their own provincial minds, they considered me an idiot.

"Just kidding, Charlie. It's not hungry," he said, between snorts. The three of them giggled like junior high girls talking with a high school hunk. "It just ate, last year." He said something in Chinese and they all burst out laughing again.

"What's so funny, Woo?"

Woo eventually settled down while the two tittering men resumed maneuvering the cart ahead and out the door. "It's not really funny, but this is the biggest snake in Taipei.

None of us thought we'd ever be so lucky to taste such a wonder. We're happy."

Addiction, I thought. Some way to get high. "What do you mean, 'it ate last year'?"

"This one eats every year or two, maybe a pig, a fawn. One big supper holds it for a long time."

I'd heard plenty about snake blood aphrodisiacs so I prepared myself to join in the fun with Woo. If I drank the blood, I would redeem myself with Meng. He probably thought I couldn't get it up last night with the girl in the "Barbershop."

He avoided serious business talk at dinner with Sun. That's why he sent Woo to get me a libido booster, a shot of self-confidence – this honor I would never refuse, no matter how woozy drinking blood might make me feel. I'd eaten weirder things, though there in the snake shop, I couldn't remember what they were. Fried ants and chocolate-covered African termites, once. Minor fare.

Woo and I entered the main room. Half the store's patrons had their arms around the snake, tugging and hoisting it onto a long wooden table. The customers or congregants – I didn't really know which but I sensed reverence within their obvious pleasure – gathered around, speaking rapidly, their voices rising. They pointed at the snake, glancing at me, everyone grinning.

"He must be twenty feet long," I said, astonished to see it stretched to full length. About ten feet from its head, a man hugged the beast against his chest, barely stretching his arms around the snake's body. "How big is he?"

Woo turned to the giant standing at the foot of the table and asked. The giant nodded, folding his hands, and stared at the animal that now lay across the table, rolling its muscles in slow shudders, aware of our attention, I thought.

One of the men picked up a pail and doused the snake with water from its tail to its head. He did it a second time. After the second pail, the snake stopped moving, except for its head that it raised and aimed straight at me.

Everyone fell still and gazed at the snake. I dragged my eyes away from it and examined the snake aficionados, trying to sense what was going on. Some stared with gleams in their eyes, others seemed to be in trances, rocking back and forth on their toes.

The giant said something to Woo. He turned to me and said, "Seven meters. Over a hundred fifty kilos. Three hundred fifty pounds, maybe more. He's in his prime. A sacrifice for every one here tonight."

The handlers stabilized the animal on the table, each man holding it in place with both of his hands. Huan motioned for me to come to him at the head of the table, where he held the sides of the snake's head between his palms. The snake kept its dull eyes fastened on me.

This animal is a god, I thought.

Woo who nodded, encouraging me to go over to Huan. Moving to the opposite end of the table, near the giant, he clutched the snake's languid tail. Huan pointed his chin first at me, then at a stainless steel pail about the size of a two-quart blender canister. As I held the pail, it reeked of organic rot and my palms squashed moist hunks of goo that stuck to its sides.

"Stand in front of the head," Woo told me. "Hold the bucket under the edge of the table. He'll chop off the head and when it drops, you catch the blood from the neck. You might need more pails." He pointed to several stainless pails stacked on a stool beside me.

"When Huan signals, take the first drink. You're the guest of honor. Then pass it around, starting with Huan."

I glanced into the faces of some of the regulars. Each one held my eyes until one of us blinked.

I felt like I was on stage with the audience of the snake blood lovers crowding closer, focusing on me and Huan and the anaconda while I stared, eyeball to eyeball with the snake. I couldn't believe how passive it was. The snake's massive strength failed it as Huan raised a cleaver in both hands, stood in a wide stance and reached as high overhead as he could.

Everyone in the room inhaled roughly as the snake opened its massive jaws and squirmed, stretching its daggery mouth toward me. Its tongue flicked out, rasping the bridge of my nose.

I jerked back from the snake's tongue. The cleaver fell, smashing into the table with a thunk. The anaconda's severed head shot up into the air, flipped over and landed, mouth agape, on the top of my head. I screamed, dropping the pail, digging the fingers of one hand into the snake's sloppy bleeding neck and pushing at its lava-hard nose with the other. The snake's jaws clenched my head, its teeth stabbing into my ears. I felt the front of my pants become wet and warm. I went blind.

Shouts in Chinese erupted and Woo screamed in English. "Charlie, wait. Stop."

Someone grabbed my hands, fighting with me to pull them away from the head. The jaws let go and the snake head rose up, scraping the back of my scalp and ripping hair out. Slime and blood flowed down my forehead and cheeks and I opened my eyes into the cold blue light of the room. I turned to find a towel to wipe off my face and slipped. My feet slid out from under me flipping me onto on my back, somehow twisted halfway under the table.

For an instant before a shower of blood sprayed my chest and face, running into my mouth, the lights dimmed and I felt myself on my back on the riverbed with Jenny lying across my legs.

I swallowed, choking on the thick warm liquid. Scrambling and flailing, I tried to stand up.

Woo screeched and suddenly the rain of blood stopped and I was three feet in the air, hanging upside from Big Man's paws. I swabbed my eyes with my sleeve and arched my neck up. Woo knelt in a shiny pool beside the table legs, his pants and shirt stained black, steadying the bucket as it filled with blood gushing from the snake's neck.

Huan stared at me, his mouth as wide open as the snake's jaws, the cleaver rebounded and raised over his head again, frozen in the air, as if he were fending off an attack.

The men holding the snake's convulsing body had their eyes closed, murmuring guttural sounds over and over. The other customers stood in shocked silence, gaping, except for a woman who had the presence of mind to snatch another pail and, standing beside Woo, waited to catch the liquid essence of the snake when Woo's pail overflowed.

The giant grunted and dropped me on my back onto one of the drinking tables, breaking the spell. The rest of the people swooped down to the floor beside the butchering table and began lapping at the puddle of blood that spread in rivulets across the tiles. Woo shouted at them but they ignored him.

Huan snatched the pail from Woo's hands and throwing his head back, he poured blood broth into his mouth, gargling before he swallowed. When he finished, blood dripping from his grinning lips, his shirt splattered, he handed the bucket to Woo.

Woo glanced at me, closed his eyes and raised the bucket to his mouth. He pulled and pulled on the blood, deep gurgling swallows. He finished, grunted and leaned back against the table, his white clothes crimsoned and soggy and offered me the pail. I raised it to my mouth and sipped.

The blood tasted like my own blood that I'd licked from cuts, but with a sweet and gamey note. It smelled a little like boiled chicken that had sat out of the refrigerator too long. I started to set the bucket on the table, but Woo signaled for me to drink more. With his head tilted to the side like a listening bird, Big Man watched me, no doubt wondering what my next move would be.

I lifted the pail up and tilted it against my lips. I opened my mouth and the warm soup surged against my throat, almost gagging me. I tipped the pail back to stop the flow and swallowed as gracefully as I could. Glancing at the giant, I saw him smile, and for good measure, I gulped again.

Everyone, except Woo and the giant and me, knelt on the floor. The snake had fallen off the table and its body lay like a fire hose, spurting gorges of blood out of its decapitated end. A man tried to prop a bucket under the gash, but he couldn't hold the snake in his blood-greased hands. Two women squatting at the shore of the scarlet blood pond used their hands to brush blood into wide-mouthed glasses, flicking the blood so quickly their fingers blurred.

Huan and Woo lunged toward me, reaching for the half-empty pail in my hands. Woo slipped and spun around, landing on his butt right at my feet. Huan glared, aghast, appealing to the giant to do something.

At the sight of Woo's pratfall, a roar of laughter erupted from my belly, convulsing my shoulders and neck. Big Man joined in, honking and huffing at the mess. Woo tried to jump up, slipped down again, and let himself fall into hilarious laughing at his predicament. The whole crowd screamed and howled. I'd never had such a good time in my life.

We pointed at each other and bayed, unable to stop. Woo finally got up and lurched over to me. "Are you okay?"

"Woo, you're crazy," I shouted. "This is what I've been waiting for all my life." I was drunk on blood and free, having a wild adventure in old Taipei.

He clapped me on the back in the first display of affection I'd ever felt from a Chinese man. "Mr. Meng was right about you." I placed the blood bucket on the floor.

Big Man handed me a towel and lumbered to the front of the store where a group had gathered outside to watch the gory melee. He shooed them away and rolled down the aluminum overhead door. Then he turned to our blood-soaked clan and muttered something. The people stopped talking.

"He told everyone 'Settle down. Stand by the wall,'" Woo said.

We all watched the giant step carefully into the bloody goo already beginning to clot into a pudding. His white suit peppered and smeared with blood. We all dreaded what could happen if he slipped onto his duff. He gracefully picked up the bucket by its handle, hefted the snake carcass onto his shoulder, laid it out straight as a post on the table, and grumbled to Huan.

Woo managed to retrieve the snake's head from the browning pool under the table. He offered it to me. The scaly flesh hung slack under dull eyes. Its jaws were jammed open showing dozens of bloody teeth with thin strings of spittle dripping from the corner of the mouth.

The strings were my hairs hanging like lo mein noodles from the decapitated head, my stomach surged and I turned away, closing my throat and holding the souring blood in my craw.

Big Man herded the other customers out of sight into the back room and returned with fresh black towels to Woo and me. Woo began stripping and told me to do the same. We swiped our bodies with the cloth, rubbing off most of the blood. A funk settled in my nose. I blew hard into the towel a half a dozen times, but the stink fruity reek of meaty decay clung inside my nostrils.

Huan had stayed at the table, blood clotting on his face and clothes, butchering the snake with the same cleaver he'd use to behead it. As I toweled the blood off my back and chest, I watched Huan slice the snake's belly and spread the skin, revealing shiny blue-gray guts. He dug his fingers in, then slipped his arm deep into the entrails and vibrated the body. When he removed his arm, he dragged out a slithery, magenta hunk of organ meat the size of a football.

Lifting the organ in both hands like priest raising a chalice, Huan called to the owner. The giant nodded impassively. Huan set the organ down on the table and cut off several finger-like chunks with quick expert slashes.

Woo whispered without moving his lips, "The liver."

Wrapped only in our towels, Woo and I approached the table along with the owner. Following Woo's lead, I picked up one of the julienned slices of anaconda liver, tipped back my head and gulped. I flashed back to the time when I was a boy and had swallowed an earthworm. The worm had been cold and rough, but the liver was warm and slipped down my throat like a smooth consommé of fresh tofu.

My snake-munching mates stood around the table, eyes closed, chewing, relishing the oily magic in their mouths. I wished I could enjoy the ceremony as much as they did. I felt a stomach spasm. The last thing I wanted to do then was to spew and lose total face with the Chinese. I shut my eyes counted my breaths, exhaling through my mouth.

When I'd calmed my guts down, I opened my eyes. All three Chinese, including the giant, sagged against the butcher table, their glazed eyes barely open.

Eventually they roused themselves and Huan slowly went back to the butchering. The giant offered Woo and me a pile of black silk which, when we unraveled it, became two huge robes, his own lounging gowns. We wound the silk around our bodies like swaddling blankets. I stepped into my shoes, squishing cool, clotting blood between my toes. Black anaconda goo spurted out of Woo's shoes. I mimicked his indifference, ignoring my last little discomfort for the sake of group unity in our Taoist bacchanal.

The giant escorted us to the front of the store and rolled up the door. He handed Woo a package and bowed. Chuckling, he shook our hands. He patted me on my head and tugged on my ears with both hands. A huge laugh erupted from his mouth, spraying drops of pink saliva into my face.

Woo and I laughed, politely, and, feeling energized, we nearly jogged back to the street where the Benz was parked, each musing to ourselves. I wiped the giant's spit off my face. A rancid, garlic smell had insinuated itself into the stench embedded in the linings of my nose.

"I never did anything like that before," I said to my groggy guide. He sprawled against the hood of the Benz. "This is the wildest night of my life.

"Nobody in all of history ever did that before," Woo said.

"I feel fine," I said, rubbing my stomach. "I never had such fun but I've been mostly a vegetarian for so long, I hope I can digest that raw meat."

"Charlie, you worry too much. The snake will take care of you."

As much as I love Chinese mysticism, I didn't want to get into any discussion of snake magic at two in the morning. A stomach I'd soothed to queasy, my head aching, I felt dizzy, my back throbbed. I just needed to get back to my room and sleep off the night of smoke and blood.

"What's in the package?" I said more to distract myself from my nausea than out of real curiosity.

"The liver for Mr. Meng."

I'd expected something like that.

"Mr. Meng gets half, Big Man gets half. They let us all

taste it. Generous. Nobody will ever taste a fifty year old snake again."

We rode in silence for a long time. I forced myself to pay strict attention to my breathing. If I let my mind stray, I knew I'd vomit snake blood all over the back seat of the Mercedes.

"That's all Big Man eats," Woo said out of the shadows. "Boa liver, viper liver, redbelly liver. He never gets soft. He can have a hundred girls and still keep going. He's number one snake man in Taiwan."

I listened without much belief or interest. Stories of the sexual powers of these men bored me. Or did they frighten me? Did these Taiwanese sublimate a boundless sex drive into their manic business dealing?

"Woo?"

One eye flickered.

"About how much does one anaconda like that cost?"

He grunted. "More than you and I have. Feeding the snake for so many years is very expensive. Big Man has always charged a premium for his skills. For us, this was a once in a lifetime chance."

How much could pigs and deer cost? I wondered. Should I ask him what all the snakes eat? I didn't want to know. What have I gotten myself into? What do I owe Meng now?

"You should know about Big Man, Charlie. He's a hero to us Taiwanese. Big Man nursed Mao Tse Tung in his last year?"

"Mao died a while ago didn't he?" I asked.

"Not too long by our standards, about thirty years," Woo said. "The president gave the Taiwanese air force permission to fly Big Man to Beijing. He kept Mao alive when doctors could barely help him breathe."

"Oh?" I said. "Did he bring snakes with him?"

"No. Beijing has good snakes. Big Man stayed a year in the Imperial Palace, treating the old man. At eighty-two, Mao died with three girls in his bed and a happy smile on his face. Before he gave up his spirit, Mao held Big Man's hand and said, 'Thank you, Big Man.'

"Mao was so grateful it's said that Big Man brought back a C-130 belly full of ancient treasures. They're in the National Museum now."

NOTE: "Blood Medicine" is a draft of a chapter included in the novel *Blood Medicine*, ©2015, Book One of the *Hour Between One and Two*, the Tofu Noir trilogy.

Skeleton Woman

What Happened to the Skeleton Woman,
the Hunter, and the Invisible Third Being

Inspired by a tale from Clarissa Pinkola Estes

1. The Skeleton Woman Returns to the Sea

Clacking, scraping, she dragged her achy bones down the woods path to the sea. Tears poured over her cracked and furrowed cheeks. Her soft blue bonnet slipped off and tangled in her shoulder blades.

Eyes, she thought, My eyes grew back. I saw the sky, the fire in his hut, the oilskin slicker he wore. I looked into his dreams. I can't stop seeing all the pain he hid from my empty head.

Exhausted, dropping down the bank, she slid out onto the mud flat.

Eyes can go. I won't need them in the dark under the water. But the heart I will miss. It appeared like a scarlet pearl, soft as a rose forming around the tiny grain of desire I kept hidden from the salt all these years.

When he reached through my ribs, his fingers probing like fearless questions, I recoiled. The moment his touch grazed the wild flesh pulsing in my chest, I looked into his shining brown eyes and I saw my true self. I collapsed. I fled to the comfort of mud.

In dim twilight, the Skeleton Woman lay tangled as a heap of old driftwood on the reeking mud flat, inviting the tide to come and scatter her across the bay.

2. The Hunter Returns to Hunting the Sea

After three days and nights, he awoke from a dreamless sleep. Lifting himself up from the icy floor of his cabin, he clutched the table, hauling his body up like the carcass of a seal.

Stumbling outside, he saw a trail scribbled in the piney woods path, a message he would never be able to read, but he understood it.

It's her, he thought. Gone back.

He loaded his boat with rope to tie her to him should he catch her, with his newest net, and with his three-pronged diamond-tipped silver narwhal hook. He tossed in an extra anchor.

His arms felt hot and numb at the same time. His fingertips were scorched. He launched into a night that his eyes saw as bright as noon because his whole body hummed with the blaze that had leapt from her heart to his. When they touched, flesh to flesh, his eyes really opened for the first time in his life. The shock of seeing his true self in her new eyes had knocked him out. Now the dim glow burned and beckoned him to the sea.

He rowed himself back and forth, dragging his net, peering into the opaque water until he nearly froze on the North Atlantic. And he came back day after day, just like always, never knowing what to expect, convinced he'd become braver.

3. The Invisible Third Being Returns to Nowhere

If you could see her, you'd see someone as large as an adult and as heavy as two bodies. But since you can't see her, you can't see that she's as small as a kitten or rabbit.

She perched in the company of owls in a pine high over the mud flats where she observed Skeleton Woman gliding peacefully under the risen tide.

Waiting patiently for days and days, she watched the Hunter strain against the waves, dragging his net through the water, tugging it in, throwing it out, pulling it up, returning to land at night with an empty face whether he caught a bass or a flounder or nothing.

The Invisible Third Being drifted down to the water where she floated behind the Hunter, almost as visible as the shadow of a drifting cormorant. One morning, as the fog lifted, she rose up with the mist, and disappeared into open sky.

That day, a mysterious fragrance perfumed the

breeze. A warm and wild scent of orchid called the Hunter ever further from shore. He caught sight of a pale blue fin rising and falling with the swells. It's her, he thought. I knew it.

He rowed on into the night.